One Snowy Night

By Jill Shalvis

Heartbreaker Bay Novels
SWEET LITTLE LIES
THE TROUBLE WITH MISTLETOE

Coming Soon:
ACCIDENTALLY ON PURPOSE

Lucky Harbor Novels
ONE IN A MILLION • *HE'S SO FINE*
IT'S IN HIS KISS • *ONCE IN A LIFETIME*
ALWAYS ON MY MIND • *IT HAD TO BE YOU*
FOREVER AND A DAY • *AT LAST*
LUCKY IN LOVE • *HEAD OVER HEELS*
THE SWEETEST THING • *SIMPLY IRRESISTIBLE*

Animal Magnetism Novels
ALL I WANT • *STILL THE ONE*
THEN CAME YOU • *RUMOR HAS IT*
RESCUE MY HEART • *ANIMAL ATTRACTION*
ANIMAL MAGNETISM

Cedar Ridge Novels
NOBODY BUT YOU • *MY KIND OF WONDERFUL*
SECOND CHANCE SUMMER

One Snowy Night

A HEARTBREAKER BAY CHRISTMAS
NOVELLA

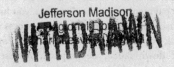
JILL SHALVIS

AVON IMPULSE

An Imprint of HarperCollins Publishers

This book is a work of fiction. References to real people, events, establishments, organizations, or locales are intended only to provide a sense of authenticity, and are used fictitiously. All other characters, and all incidents and dialogue, are drawn from the author's imagination and are not to be construed as real.

Chapter One

CHRISTMAS EVE HAD the nerve to show up just like it did every year: way too quickly and with ridiculous fanfare.

The nerve.

Rory Andrews stood in the courtyard of the Pacific Pier Building in San Francisco, surrounded by sparkly holiday lights and enough garlands to give the place its own ozone, and told herself things could be worse.

She just wasn't sure how.

It was the unknown, she decided. Because this year, unlike the past six, she'd be spending Christmas with her family, a thought that caused a swarm of butterflies to take flight in her belly.

Not an uncommon feeling since she'd turned twenty-three a few months back and decided it was time to become a person she could be proud of if it killed her. And given the guy leaning against one of the lamp poles clearly waiting for her, arms crossed, frown in place, it just might.

Max Stranton. At his side sat Carl, his huge, eternally hungry, adorable Doberman.

"No," she said, not to Carl but to Carl's owner. Who was not lovable. "No way."

As always when their gazes locked, Max's was a disconcerting mix of heat and . . . something else that she couldn't quite figure out, as he was good at hiding when he wanted to be. She never quite knew how to take the heat because it seemed reluctant. He was attracted to her but didn't want to be.

Ditto. He made her knees wobble. And also a couple of other inner reactions that shouldn't be happening in public.

"Merry Christmas to you too, Rory," he said, and damn. It wasn't just his eyes. His voice was rough and sexy, and for that matter, so was the rest of him.

He worked for an investigations and security firm in the building. Basically he and the rest of his team were fixers and finders for hire. To say that Max was good at his job was an understatement. He stood there looking like sex on a stick with a duffle bag slung over a broad shoulder, his dark hair two weeks past needing a cut, and the icy wind of an incoming storm plastering his clothes to a body that could be registered as a lethal weapon.

"What are you doing here?" she asked calmly even if her heart was anything but, pounding all the way up to her throat and ears because she knew. She knew *exactly* why he was here. "I don't need a ride home."

A flash of wry humor slid in with all that sizzling heat. "Because you'd rather take two buses and a train than get into my truck with me?" he asked.

Well yes, actually.

Living and working in San Francisco was a dream come true for her. She'd turned her life around in the past few years but she still had some deep regrets, one of them being how she'd run away at age seventeen. This was something her wonderful but nosy boss Willa had talked her into facing once and for all, so she'd called home. She'd promised her stepdad she'd come for Christmas to surprise her mom and three half sisters. He'd expressed surprise and then doubt, both with good reason.

Rory had made promises to come home before, and . . . hadn't. Every time she'd flaked. It'd been fear and anxiety, but she was ready to face all that now and she'd told him so. She'd even offered to pick up the gift he'd ordered for her mom from the city and get it home before dawn on Christmas morning.

If she managed to do so, all would be forgiven.

Not that he'd said so in those words, but she felt the pressure all the same. She wanted to do this; she was ready to do this.

"It's Christmas Eve," Max said now, keys in hand. "I just finished a job. I'm leaving to spend a few days with my family. I'm going right past your mom's house."

Which was in Tahoe, where Max had also been raised—four hours north in good weather, which wasn't going to be tonight. Her stomach jangled. Fate or Karma or whatever was in charge of such things was a cruel master, having her first crush of all people, the *one* guy on the entire planet who made her feel like that young, neglected, bullied, unwanted teen all over again, be the only smart ride home tonight.

Max's body language said he was relaxed and laid-back as he watched her think too much, but she knew better. He spent most of his days rooting out the asshats of San Francisco. He was a chameleon when he wanted to be, a sharp one. Nothing got by him.

Well, except one thing, of course—he had no idea that once upon a time for her the sun had risen and set on his smile. She'd flown under the radar in high school. Hell, she'd flown under the radar in life, and she'd been really good at it. Plus Max had never had a shortage of girls who were interested in him so he'd had no reason to look past any of the ones throwing themselves at his feet in order to see her.

But that was then. In the here and now, things felt . . . different. Whether either of them wanted to admit it or not, they'd taken notice of each other, and even more unbelievably, she often caught him watching her with what felt like heat and desire.

Not that he'd ever made a move.

"Are you ready?" he asked.

The ten-million-dollar question. "As I'll ever be," she said.

"I don't get it." His tone was age-old male bafflement with a dash of annoyance. His eyes were a very dark shade of green. They looked almost black now in the night. "I had to find out from Willa that you needed a ride. You could've asked me yourself. You should have asked me, Rory."

Right. Because they talked so much. But before she could say that, or even pet Carl, her favorite dog on the planet, a woman ran out of the convenience store on the corner, breathless and adorable in a red apron and Santa hat.

"Just wanted to tell you something," she said to Max and flung herself into his arms.

He had little choice but to catch her, and she laughed and kissed him, taking her time about it too.

While they were lip-locked, Carl gave one deep bark and the woman finally pulled back, grinning wide as she said to both man and his dog, "Merry Christmas! See you next year!"

And then she vanished back into the store where she worked, which Rory knew because she often bought ice cream there after a long day at work.

Max shook his head but was looking amused. Rory searched his gaze, looking to see if Santa's Helper caused that same breathless heat she'd gotten used to seeing when he looked at *her*.

It wasn't there.

She took a deep breath at that, not wanting to acknowledge it as relief. She shouldn't care that he hadn't felt an overwhelming hunger for that girl.

"Let's do this," he said.

"This" of course being the unwelcome chore of giving her a ride. "Look, I'm not sure this is a good idea." Because honestly? Two buses and a train would be a piece of cake in comparison, never mind that she didn't have the money for that.

"Rory," he said, a hint of impatience in his tone.

Once again she looked into his eyes, and at what she saw, her heart stopped on a dime.

The heat was back. For her.

"This isn't exactly my idea of fun either," he said. "Trust me."

Ha. She wasn't exactly on the trust program with any man but especially not this one. Not that she was about to tell *him* that.

Max's attention was suddenly drawn to the alley and the man standing in it. Old Man Eddie was a fixture of the Pacific Pier Building every bit as much as the fountain in the center of the courtyard. Everyone who worked here did their best to take care of him, including Rory.

"Hold on a sec," Max said and moved toward Eddie, who was wearing a sweatshirt with a peace sign and Hawaiian-print board shorts, his medical marijuana card laminated and hanging from a lanyard around his neck.

"Merry Christmas, man," Rory heard Max say and then he slipped the old man something that she suspected was cash.

And damn if her heart didn't execute a slow roll in her chest, softening for him, which didn't exactly make her night.

Old Man Eddie pocketed the money and grinned at Max, and then they did one of those male hugs that involved back slapping and some complicated handshake.

Ignoring them, Rory reached into her bag and pulled

out some red ribbon. A big part of her job at South Bark Mutt Shop was grooming. Carl had been her first client earlier that morning and afterward, she'd woven a piece of the festive ribbon around his collar, which he'd seemed to love, but there was no ribbon in sight now. Crouching in front of him, she replaced it, looping it in a jaunty bow at the side of his neck. "There," she said. "Better, right? The girls'll be falling all over themselves to get you."

Carl gave her a big, slurpy lick along her chin. Then he nosed her bag, sniffing out the fact that she had goodies in there. "Later," she promised.

"No," Max said, coming back to them. "Hell no. Take that thing off, you're going to kill his image."

Rory rose to her full height, which still wasn't even close to Max's. She barely made it up to his shoulder and, dammit, she wished she was in heels. "A ribbon doesn't emasculate him, and even if it did, there's nothing wrong with that."

"Of course there's not," he said. "But female or male, he's a working dog and in our business he—or *she*—has to be tough and badass. A bow doesn't exactly say 'stop and drop or I'll *make* you stop and drop.'"

Okay, so maybe he had a point there. "It's Christmas Eve," she said. "I think he can take the night off of being tough and badass, can't he?"

Max blew out a sigh that spoke volumes on what he thought of the matter—and her—and headed for the wrought iron gate to the street, stopping to hold it open for her.

As she passed through, their bodies brushed together,

his hard as stone and yet somehow also deliciously warm, and hers . . . softened. There was no other word for it.

At the contact, he sucked in a breath and jerked her gaze to his. And then she was sucking in a breath too, frozen in place, held there by the shocking chemistry that always seemed to sizzle between them, just under the surface.

She had no idea what to do with that, but damn . . .

Max muttered something to himself about bad timing and idiocy before leading her to his truck, parked at the curb.

Which brought up the question—just how badly did she want to get home? Bad, she could admit. She needed to make amends. She needed forgiveness for being such a horrible, unhappy, terrible teenager, even if it meant swallowing her pride and taking the ride from Max.

She got into the truck in tune to a growing wind and a clap of thunder in the far distance. Max settled Carl in the backseat and then leaned in to buckle him in, giving the big dog an 'ol kiss on the snout as he did. The unexpected action was such a sweet, gentle thing to do, and such a dichotomy from his usual stoic badassery that Rory found herself smiling.

Max caught her expression as he slid in behind the wheel. "What?" he asked.

"What what?" she asked.

"You're smiling."

"Is there a law against that?"

He put his truck in gear and pulled out into the street. "No, but you don't usually aim it at me."

"You've got that backward, don't you?" she asked, deciding not to mention that she'd been aiming the smile at Carl.

Max slid her a look that sizzled her nerve endings and then redirected his attention to the streets. San Francisco was looking pretty gorgeous in her Christmaswear, a myriad of lights decorating the buildings, light poles wrapped in garlands. As they made their way through the busy district and got on the freeway, it began to rain. Hard.

The sound of the rain pinging off the truck was loud, echoing in the interior. Max didn't speak and she blew out a breath. It was going to be a long ride home. *Home.* Just the word brought more than a few nerves. And nerves made her babble. "So what's your problem with me?"

Nothing from Max but a slight tightening of his scruffy jaw.

"Can't decide on one thing?" she asked.

"I don't have a problem."

Okaaaay. She searched for something to else say, anything at all to draw him out because the silence was going to drive her batty. "Heard you guys had to jump off the roof of a building to catch some bad guys for the good guys yesterday."

He smiled at the memory as if it'd been fun. "Can't talk about work," he said.

Right. "So who's the chick who tried to swallow your tongue?"

He choked out a laugh but didn't speak, which just plain old pissed her off. She knew damn well he could talk; she'd seen him do it plenty. But he absolutely wasn't interested in conversation with her. Fine. Point served, silence it was. She went with it for all of three minutes, but in the end she couldn't do it. Turning in her seat, she studied her driver.

Tall, hard, and lean, he'd definitely changed since they'd gone to high school together. She'd left home immediately after her junior year. She'd eventually gotten a job and taken her GED but she hadn't kept up with anyone from Tahoe. Mostly because she'd had such a crap time growing up. She'd needed to get away with a clean slate, badly, and frankly there'd been no one she'd wanted to stay in touch with.

Except maybe . . . secretly . . . Max himself, a fact she'd take to her grave, thank you very much. They'd had a science class together, that was it; nothing memorable for him, she was certain. But he'd been kind to her, twice taking her on as a lab partner when no one else had wanted the shy, bad-at-science wallflower, and she'd never been able to forget it. Or him. "So what college did you end up at?" she asked.

Surprisingly enough, *this* got her a reaction. He looked at her across the dark console, rain and wind and city lights slashing as harshly across his features as his voice sounded when he asked, *"Are you kidding me?"*

Chapter Two

MAX HADN'T MEANT to respond to Rory's questions at all but that last one—*where had he gone to college?*—cut through all his good intentions and lit the fuse of his rare temper.

She couldn't be serious. She knew damn well what she'd done to him, what she'd cost him.

She had to.

Didn't she?

He glanced at her, and the intensity that was always between them ratcheted up a notch, something he'd have sworn wasn't possible.

"Why would I be kidding you?" she asked.

Like he was going to go there with her, but at whatever was in his expression along with the tone of his voice, Carl whined.

Rory narrowed her eyes at Max, clearly blaming him for upsetting the dog, before she twisted, going up on her knees to reach over the back of her seat for Carl.

His dog, hampered by his seatbelt, whined again and leaned into her touch.

Rory made a soft sound in her throat and clicked out of her seatbelt to wrap her arms around the big oaf—a fact Max knew only because he could see her both in his rearview mirror and over his shoulder. He watched as she loved up on his big, slobbery dog, not seeming to care one little bit when Carl smiled and drooled all over her pretty sweater.

Most women didn't like Carl.

Which didn't matter in the least to Max. Women came and went, if he was very lucky. And yeah, he'd been luckier than most in that regard. But there'd been no keepers, much to his family's ever loving dismay. So far, Carl was his only keeper.

And Carl clearly loved and adored Rory.

That wasn't the problem. Nope, the problem was that Rory seemed completely clueless to what she'd done to Max. She'd ruined his life and she'd either forgotten or she didn't care. The crazy thing was that he'd hardly known her. The only reason he'd even known her name was because he'd been her lab partner a few times. But though he'd enjoyed her company, she'd ignored him outside of class.

And back then she hadn't been his type anyway. He'd been an unapologetic jock, and he'd be the first to admit that he'd been enough of an ass to enjoy the perks of that—including going out with girls known to enjoy sleeping with the most popular athletes.

He glanced in the rearview mirror again. Huge mistake. All he could see was Rory's heart-stopping ass covered in snug, faded denim that outlined her every curve, and his mouth actually watered, wanting to bite it.

In the time that they'd both been working in the city, he'd come to realize that not only had she outgrown her shyness, but she was smart, resourceful, and funny. If he didn't resent their past so much, he'd probably have asked her out a long time ago.

But he did resent their past, which left him both driven nuts by her presence and also somehow . . . hungry for her. Which meant it was official: he'd lost his mind.

If he'd ever had it in the first place.

He glanced at the very nice view again and the wheels of his truck hit the edge of his lane, giving off a loud whump whump whump. "Shit," he muttered and jerked the truck back into the lane.

Smooth, real smooth, he thought with self-disgust.

At the motion of his truck swerving, Rory nearly slid into his lap.

"Sorry," she gasped, bracing one hand on his shoulder, the other high up on his thigh, using them to shove clear of him.

He could still feel the heat of her hands on him as she flopped back in her seat, hair in her face. She shoved it clear and then bent over and started rifling through the huge purse at her feet.

The movement slid her sweater north and her jeans south, revealing a two-inch strip of the creamy white skin of her lower back.

And two matching dimples that made his mouth water again.

"What the hell are you doing?" he managed to ask.

"Nothing." She straightened, coming up with a dog biscuit, which she tossed back to Carl. The dog snapped it out of thin air, practically swallowing it whole, and then licked his chops.

"You carry bones with you?" he asked in surprise.

"Of course," she said, like *didn't everyone?*

His phone buzzed an incoming call. He answered it via speaker but before he could say a word, his elder, know-it-all sister Cass spoke.

"I know you're on your way," she said, her voice blaring out from his truck's speakers. "So I'll be quick. Two things. One, the weather is atrocious and the roads up here are an epic disaster already so please be careful, and two, don't forget that we've got a promise between us."

"Cass—"

"No excuses," she said. "The next girl you feel something for, anything at all, you have to go for it, no exceptions. That's my Christmas present and I just wanted to remind you of that. And since I'm assuming you're going to say you've felt nothing, you should know I've got you covered."

Max didn't bother to groan. Nor did he look at Rory, who he could sense straightening in her seat with interest. "What have you done, Cass?"

"Me?" she asked innocently. "Nothing."

Yeah, and he was Santa Claus. "*Cass.*"

Her sigh echoed in the truck interior. "Okay, fine, I might have invited a friend—"

"No," he said.

"Come on. Kendall's cute, smart, gainfully employed, and she has a crush on your dog."

"How the hell does she know Carl?"

"Honestly, Max? Are you seriously not reading my Facebook messages?"

No. He wasn't.

"I started a Facebook page for Carl weeks ago," Cass said. "He's already got a thousand likes."

If he hadn't been driving into a downpour with hurricane-force winds, he might've taken his hands off the wheel to rub his temples where a headache was forming. "I'm disconnecting you now," he warned, ignoring Rory's snort.

"So that's a yes on Kendall, right?"

"It's a firm *hell no*," he said.

Cass was silent a beat, thinking. Never a good thing for Max. "So . . . there *is* someone you're feeling something for," she said.

He nearly laughed. Yes. Yes, he was feeling something for the woman sitting next to him but it sure as hell wasn't what Cass was hoping for.

"Even a little spark of attraction counts," Cass warned. "You promised, Max. And you never break promises."

True story. He never broke promises.

"Max? Is there someone, then?"

Max slid a gaze across the console and found Rory staring at him, her dark brown eyes swirling with emotions that he couldn't possible put a finger on without a full set of directions. She was beautiful in the girl-next-door way, meaning she had absolutely zero idea of her own power. In fact, Rory had always seemed completely oblivious of her looks. In high school, she'd been thin but had worn clothes that had tended toward shapeless, which had allowed her to be invisible as she'd clearly liked to be. She was still thin but had acquired curves in all the right places now, shown off by clothes that actually fit her. Her long hair was wavy and had its own mind. She hadn't tried to tame it, letting it flow in dark brown waves to her breasts. If she was wearing makeup, he couldn't see any.

What he had no problem seeing was her interest in his response to his sister.

Okay, yes, so he felt a physical attraction to her. And he'd felt that response more than once. A lot more, if he was being honest with himself, but he'd hidden it. Or so he hoped, telling himself it was nothing more than a natural male response to a female form. That was it. Because he wasn't attracted to Rory—unless you count the attraction of strangling her.

He shifted, knowing he was lying to himself.

"Max?" Cass asked.

"Bad reception," he said and disconnected the call, understanding damn well he'd pay for that later.

Rory snorted, amused.

He ignored that and her, and concentrated on the roads. Which were indeed shit.

"You could've told her about Santa's Helper, your girlfriend from the convenience store," Rory said casually.

He slid her a quick look. "Tabby's not my girlfriend," he said.

"So you kiss all the store clerks then?"

He rolled his eyes. He and Tabby weren't complicated. They were friends, with the very occasional added "benefits," but neither of them were interested in more. "Tabby's not in the picture."

"Does *she* know that?"

"Here's an idea," he said. "How about you make it my Christmas present to stop with the twenty questions?"

She turned to the window, shoulders squared.

Ah, hell. Now he felt like an asshole, but he had to admit, he did appreciate the silence.

About an hour up the highway, the rain turned to slush. He knew it wouldn't be much longer before they hit snow, which didn't bother him any. He'd grown up driving off-road vehicles and boats, and his dad often proudly said Max could drive a semi into an asscrack. And it was true, he could drive anything anywhere under any conditions. Where the danger and unknown came in was from the other idiots on the road.

Luckily tonight there was a shortage of them. They had the roads to themselves, probably because only the hearty would even dare try to be out in this insanity.

At the halfway mark, he stopped for fuel. Before he pumped gas, he tried to take Carl out, wanting him to do his business now so they wouldn't have to make another stop. "Let's go."

Carl curled up tight on his seat, eyes closed, playing possum. Carl didn't like snow very much. Max looked at Rory.

Rory shrugged.

"Come on," he said to Carl. "This'll be your last chance for a few hours."

Nothing from Carl.

"Now," Max said.

Carl, still not opening his eyes, only growled low in his throat.

From the passenger seat, Rory chuckled. "Is it like looking in a mirror?" she asked.

"Funny." Except not. He lowered his face to the dog's. "If you get up right this minute, I've got a doggie cookie—"

Before he'd even finished the sentence, Carl jumped up and out of the truck without a backward glance. "How about you?" he asked Rory. "You need a pit stop?"

She looked out the window into the snowy mess. "I'm good."

"Not even for a doggie cookie?"

She smiled but shook her head.

Whatever. Not his problem.

She did, however, try to give him cash for gas when he came back with Carl, which Max flatly refused. He knew she was strapped, that she barely made ends meet. He also knew he was lucky as hell to have a great job with great pay, and yeah, that great pay was because his job could be dangerous, but he was good at what he did. And even if he hadn't landed a great job that he loved, he had his family. The entire nosy bunch would do anything for him and he knew it.

Rory didn't have that kind of support. She'd had it rough growing up. Her dad had never been around and her mom had remarried when Rory had been young. Her stepdad was a good guy, but 100 percent no-nonsense. He could be a real hard-ass, a stickler for obedience and all that. Rory had three half sisters, all sweet kids but quiet and meek.

Rory was the opposite of quiet and meek, and she hadn't fit in. As far as he knew, she'd left school after their junior year and had never been back. And after what she'd done to him, he'd told himself he'd been more than fine with that.

But it didn't mean that he hadn't worried more than a little bit. Or that he wasn't aware of how hard it was for her to make it on her own, in San Francisco no less, a very expensive city. She worked at South Bark Mutt Shop and she also went to night school, and he knew she lived with a couple of roommates and still barely made ends meet. He didn't like to think about how she must struggle just to keep food in her belly. So no, he wasn't about to take her damn gas money.

He'd just started pumping the gas when his phone buzzed an incoming call. Willa ran South Bark and was Rory's boss. She was also the one who'd asked him to give Rory a ride to Tahoe, clearly having no idea that Max and Rory had gone to school together and had history. A bad history.

"How's the ride going?" Willa asked.

Max leaned against his truck. "Well, we haven't killed each other yet."

Willa didn't laugh.

"You know I'm kidding, right?" *Sort of . . .*

"Max." Willa's voice was quiet. Serious. "There are things I probably should've told you about Rory."

"You mean about the chip on her shoulder?" he asked wryly. "Yeah, I'm aware."

"She's earned that chip, Max. The hard way."

"And let me guess. You're going to fill me in."

"She's smart, so smart, Max. She'll fool you if you let her."

He shook his head and hunkered beneath the overhang, trying to avoid getting snow in his face while he waited for his gas tank to fill. "What does that even mean?"

"She's been with me for six years—"

"Working in your shop, I know," he said, impatient to get out of the snow, back in the truck and on the road.

"But what you don't know is how she came to me."

Actually, he did. Rory had pretty much ran away from home and—

"It was late one night," Willa said. "I was on a walk through the Marina Green when I found a girl in the park, sick as a dog from a drug someone had dumped in her drink."

Max froze. This was something he didn't know, although he wished he had because he'd have gladly hunted down the asshole who'd drugged her and he'd have—

"I'm not telling you this to make you mad," Willa said quietly. "I just want you to understand the chip."

He let out a long, purposeful breath. "What happened?"

"I took her to the hospital, helped her recover from

events that she can't remember to this day, and gave her a job. But it wasn't easy. It took her a long time to learn to trust me."

Imagining what she must've suffered and reeling from that, Max couldn't even speak.

"Basically, I bullied her back to life," Willa said. "And lately she's been really . . . okay. Even happy."

Max knew this to be true. He'd seen Rory in the courtyard of their building, smiling and laughing with friends. He'd seen her with the animals in Willa's shop, specifically with Carl, who loved and adored her. And the reason he kept seeing her was because in spite of himself, he'd been drawn to her and he'd made sure their paths crossed. Often.

Shit.

He peered inside his truck, expecting to see Rory hunched over her phone, but there was no phone in sight. Instead she had her head bent to his dog, who was in her lap. All 100 plus pounds of him, big head on her shoulder.

He went back to the overhang. "Why are you telling me all this?" he asked Willa.

"Because I know there's something between you. A chemistry. We've all seen it, Max, the way you come by the shop with Carl for more groomings than you need, making sure to do it when Rory is there."

"Maybe I just love my stupid dog," he said, not happy to hear that he'd been that transparent when it came to his uncomfortable and complicated feelings for Rory.

"Oh, I know that's also true," Willa said smugly. "But that's not why you tip her so much. Look, I can tell by your tone I'm annoying you, so let me make it count. I know that you're trustworthy or you wouldn't be working for Archer. I guess I'm just hoping you can also be . . . gentle."

Max pressed his thumbs into his eye sockets. "Willa—"

"I know. You're big and badass and tough, and I get it, you don't do gentle. But maybe, for Rory, you could try."

Once again he looked in the truck. Rory was talking to Carl, smiling while she was at it. But once upon a time, not so long ago, she'd been hurt. Badly. And that killed him. *Fuck.* "Yeah. I guess I could try."

He heard Willa suck in a breath clogged with emotion. "Merry Christmas, Max," she said softly. "You deserve it."

Actually, there was someone who deserved it far more and the hell of it was, it was the last person he'd expected it to be, and she was sitting in his truck hugging his big, silly dog.

Chapter Three

WHEN MAX OPENED the truck door a few minutes later and found Carl in his seat, he gave the dog a long look.

Carl hefted out a huge sigh and got into the back.

"Thank you, Carl," Rory said pointedly with a glance at Max that said he was clearly an idiot.

Max was an indeed an idiot, but not for not thanking his dog.

He was going to do as Willa had asked. He was going to be . . . *Christ* . . . gentle, even if it killed him. And it might. He was also going to get his own emotions under control, because at the moment he was filled with a cold fury over what Rory had suffered and he had nowhere to vent it.

"You were on the phone," Rory said.

"I was."

She looked at him, clearly waiting for more, her pretty eyes not giving much away. She was so petite a good wind could blow her away, but that analogy implied she was fragile.

Rory was anything but fragile, and in fact her inner strength was even more attractive to him than her beauty.

"It was Willa," he said, willing to give her that. Besides she was more curious than a cat and he wanted to appease that curiosity and fast, before she figured out the rest.

She looked at him, surprised. "What did she want?"

Shit. On top of curious as a cat, she was like Carl with a damn bone. He twisted around to buckle Carl back in and then put on his own seatbelt. He turned the engine over and cranked up the radio.

Rory turned it off. "She already made you drive me, so what now?"

"Nothing."

Rory turned in her seat to fully face him. "Was she checking to see if we'd killed each other?"

He smiled at that, a thought that had been so close to his own, but she narrowed her eyes, not amused. "What did she want, Max?"

He went to put the truck in gear but she leaned into him to turn off the engine and grab his keys. Her breast brushed against his arm, giving him another zap of awareness.

"Come on," she said. "This is Willa we're talking about. I love her, but she's incapable of not sticking her nose in where it doesn't belong, especially when it comes to me. What did she want?"

Shit, it'd been two minutes and he was already regretting his "gentle" promise. He looked her right in the eyes. "Nothing."

Her eyes went to little slits. "Liar." She opened her door, revealing that the slush had turned to snow, as she swung his keys from her fingers. "Tell me or say goodbye to your keys."

"That'll strand you too," he pointed out.

She raised her eyebrows and he got the message. She didn't care.

"Fine," he said. "She told me to be nice to you. Actually, she said gentle." While she gaped at that, he snagged the keys from her lax fingers, feeling like an asshole when he leaned into her, reaching past her to slam her door shut.

She didn't shrink back, which meant that their bodies once again bumped up against each other, and it was like they knew what his brain couldn't seem to comprehend—he wanted her. He was a little thrown by that, and the now familiar zing of electricity, only slightly mollified to realize by the way her breath hitched that she felt it too.

"If you even try to be *gentle*," she said, "I'll get out and walk."

He pinched the bridge of his nose and laughed. He couldn't help it. She drove him insane. "Got it."

"I mean it."

"I believe you."

"Good," she said, sounding only slightly appeased. "Now tell me what she told you to make you agree to such a thing."

Christ, she was good. "How do you know she told me anything?"

"Again, it's Willa," she said. She crossed her arms and stared at him, and for a second he was pretty sure she could see right inside his head and read his mind. "She told you something to make you feel sorry for me," she guessed.

He schooled his features into a blank face, or so he hoped. "I don't feel sorry for you," he said.

"Ha!" she cried, pointing at him. "She did! What was it? That I applied for an internship at a local vet, which I need for the animal tech credential I want, and got turned down flat for lack of credible references?"

Shit. No, he hadn't known that and his heart twisted for her. "Why didn't you ask someone to give you a reference?" he asked. "Archer, Joe, Spence, Finn . . . me? Any one of us would've jumped to help you."

She hadn't taken her eyes off of him. "Okay," she said slowly. "So it wasn't that."

Yeah, this conversation was about to go south fast. He reached to start the engine again because no way did he want this little guessing game to take a dark turn, which it would if she landed on the truth.

"There was only one other thing she could've told you that would have made you feel sorry enough for me to give me a ride," she said, staring at him. "But if she'd told you that, I think I'd be able to tell."

He met her gaze and she gasped softly, her eyes holding his prisoner. "Oh my God," she whispered, leaning back away from him. "Damn her."

"You were attacked in the park when you first landed in San Francisco," he said quietly, finding it a shocking effort to keep his voice calm. "That shouldn't have happened to you. It shouldn't happen to *anyone*."

She turned away. "We're not discussing this."

"Did you press charges?"

She looked out into the starry night. "Drive."

"Rory, please tell me he's rotting in a jail cell."

"Drive, dammit."

"Hang on a sec—"

"I didn't press charges and he's not rotting in a jail cell because I don't remember what he looks like!" she burst out. "I accepted a drink from a stranger, he drugged me, and I remember nothing. Not his face, not anything about him, and not a single second of that night at all. So no, I didn't turn him in. I had nothing to turn in. I was an idiot, okay? I was a complete idiot and I paid the price, and now if you don't mind, I don't want to talk about it ever again."

"I get that, but—"

"Not. Ever. Again," she said tightly. "And I mean it, Max. Bring it up and I'm out. I'll walk to Tahoe, I don't care." She turned to him then, eyes blazing with strength and temper. "We clear?"

Her strength was . . . amazing. "Crystal," he said quietly.

She nodded and relaxed marginally. "Good. And one more thing. If you so much as try to be gentle or handle me with kid gloves, I'll kick your ass. And I could do it too—your boss taught me some mean moves."

He believed her. If Archer had taught her then she was lethal, and he was glad for it. No one would take advantage of her again. He started the truck and navigated their way through the falling snow back onto the highway, where they left most of civilization behind as they hit the wild Sierras.

It was always a surreal thing to drive in heavy snow in the dark of night. In the black landscape, the snow came at them in diagonal slashing lines across the windshield. The road narrowed to two lanes, winding back and forth in tight S-turns as they began to climb the summit.

They hadn't seen another car in miles when Rory started to wriggle in her seat.

"What's the matter?" he asked, not taking his eyes off the road to look at her. It was always best to not look at her because doing so messed with his head in ways he couldn't begin to explain.

"I've got to make a pit stop," she said.

For this he took his gaze off the road and stared at her in disbelief. "I just asked you if you had to go. While we were at the damn gas station."

"That was thirty minutes ago. And I didn't have to go then." She glanced back at Carl. "He has to go again too."

Bullshit. But as if on cue, Carl whined softly.

Hell. Max gestured to the scene in front of them. Nothing but thick, unforgiving forestland. "Where would you like to stop?"

"At a bathroom."

He let out a short laugh. "Okay, princess. I'll just wave my magic wand and make one appear."

She wriggled some more. "Fine. I'll make do. Pull over anywhere, I guess."

"Serious?"

"As a heart attack," she said. "Unless you're not fond of your leather seats?"

He pulled over and together they peered out the windows to the endless sea of woods. "Pick a tree," he said. "Any tree. Make it close to the road because I don't have any snowshoes in the truck."

"I'm not going to pee close to the road."

"Unless you want to wade in up to your cute ass and swim through the accumulation of snow in those woods, that's exactly what you're going to do."

Rory blew out a sigh, zipped up her jacket, and pulled the hood over her head. She opened her door and Carl leapt out ahead of her. She let out a low laugh and then hesitated.

"What?" Max asked.

"Do you think there are bears out there?"

He eyed the foot of fresh snow, still coming down sideways in the vicious wind. "I don't think there's *anything* out there tonight."

"I bet you're just saying that," she said. "You probably *want* a bear to get me."

"I don't want a bear to get you." He didn't. But he wouldn't mind if, say, she stood beneath a tree and it unloaded snow on her . . .

She blinked into the night. "Where did Carl go?"

"Probably to do his business." He hopped out too. "Carl!"

Nothing but the sound of the wind beating up the trees two hundred feet above them. The heavy snow continued to fall but it did so with an eerie, ominous silence.

Shit. "Wait here," he said. "I've got a flashlight in the back."

"I've got a flashlight too—"

"Mine's better."

"How do you know?" she asked, sounding insulted.

"I just do."

"Are you always so obnoxiously stubborn—"

He ignored the rest of that sentence, knowing she couldn't find Carl with the flashlight app on her phone. He dug and came up with his big Maglite, turned back and . . . nearly plowed Rory over because she was standing right there, close, like she'd been snugged up to his back, afraid of the dark. He grabbed her, slipping an arm around her to steady her. "Sorry—"

Sorry nothing. Because she was soft and smelled good and she stood there, right there, with . . . a decent-sized Maglite of her own in one hand, Carl obedient and smiling at her other side.

"Got him," she said sweetly.

Like she was sweet. He knew damn well she was smart as hell, she was resourceful, a survivor . . . She was a *lot* of things, but sweet wasn't one of them.

Then she crouched down and hugged Carl. "Good boy. You were just checking for snakes, weren't you? Such a good, pretty, wonderful boy."

Carl panted happily and set his big head on her shoulder, the ungrateful bastard. They were both covered in snow. Hell, they all were.

While Rory made her way behind a tree, Max dried Carl off and got him into the truck. When Rory came out of the woods, Max really wanted not to care that she was wearing more snow than clothes and shivering, but he couldn't do it. He watched while with shaking hands she carefully shook off before climbing into the truck. Then she stripped out of her jacket that clearly wasn't water-proof.

This left her in a soft off-white sweater that was damp and clinging to her like a second skin. She wore a white lace bra, also damp, and not doing much to hide the fact that she truly was cold. And he was absolutely concen-trating on that and how she looked like she needed a hot cheeseburger, and *not* her nipples, two hard little beads threatening to poke through both the lace and the mate-rial of her sweater.

Had he thought of her as the sweet, girl-next-door type? Maybe if the girl next door was pinup material, be-cause *damn*. Sitting there with her long waves clinging to her face and shoulders and chest, giving him peekaboo glimpses of her perfect breasts, he couldn't remember why he didn't like her and didn't want to like her.

"What?" she said, wrapping her arms around herself. "You've never seen cold nipples before?"

Yes, but not ones that made his mouth water to taste. Kiss. Nibble. Suck into his mouth . . . "Did you see any bears?"

Rolling her eyes, she pulled a hair tie from around her wrist and used it to contain the wet mass of waves on top of her head.

He handed her a towel, but she shook her head. "I'm fine."

"Yeah, if *fine* is drenched and cold," he said. "Take it. It's not the same one I used on Carl."

"I wouldn't care about that," she said. "But you might have to stop and put on chains soon and you'll need a towel for yourself."

"We're not going to need chains," he said. "I'm in four-wheel drive and we've got good tires. Now use the damn towel, you're dripping all over the place."

As he knew it would, this galvanized her into action and she ran the towel over herself in jerky motions. When she was done, she was still shivering, and after a hesitation, she pulled off her damp sweater.

This left her in a white camisole and aforementioned white lace bra, neither of which were all that significant.

"You going to stare at me all night or get us back on the road?" she asked coolly.

Gentle . . . With that word echoing in his head, he aimed the heater vents her way and pulled them back onto the highway.

Things had gone downhill in the few minutes they'd been stopped. The snow was really accumulating now, making the highway slick, forcing him to slow down. Way down.

"At this rate, it's gonna take all night to get there," she said, sounding worried.

Most likely she didn't want to spend any more time with him than necessary. But it wasn't like this was how he'd seen himself spending Christmas Eve either.

In the very loud silence of the truck, his belly grumbled, reminding him he'd missed dinner. And lunch.

He'd had breakfast but it felt like it'd been days since then.

He heard Rory rustling around and ignored her until a sandwich appeared beneath his nose. "No, thanks," he said.

"*Take it.*"

"I'm good."

"Yeah, well, your stomach says otherwise," she said.

"I'm not eating *your* food," he said, refusing to take the dinner she'd so clearly packed for herself.

She let out a sound of female frustration. "Tell me something. Are you *always* this stubborn or is it something special you save just for me?"

"I meant I'm not eating *your* dinner," he clarified.

"I learned how to share in kindergarten. You should try it sometime."

He blew out a sigh. "Fine. I'll take half if you eat the other half."

She looked surprised and then shrugged. "Deal."

Starving to the bone, he wolfed through his portion of her admittedly delicious PB&J and then watched as she ate only half of her half, and then gave the last quarter to Carl.

His heart squeezed as Carl chomped his portion down in one bite, licked his huge chops, and gave her an adoring gaze.

Rory laughed and then pulled something else from her bag of magic tricks—a thermos.

"Hot chocolate," she said, pouring Max half of what she had. "Careful, it's still hot."

"Thanks." He'd known he'd be making this drive tonight and he hadn't given provisions a single thought. After all, he had an emergency kit in the back and he was good.

But she was better. She'd clearly given this lots of thought and was prepared, and it made him wonder why she was going home in the first place. He knew she hadn't been there in years. "I was surprised to find that you were going to Tahoe," he said, fishing.

She sipped her hot chocolate. "Should've packed marshmallows," she murmured.

He had the oddest urge to stop and get her some but they were nowhere near a store.

She drained her cup and had a chocolate mustache. Her tongue came out and licked her lips with great relish and he nearly ran them off the road.

Startled, she glanced over at him.

He stared resolutely straight ahead at the road—or what he could see of it—wondering what the hell this odd reaction to her was. Uncalled for. Stupid. *Very* stupid.

"You okay?" she asked.

"Terrific. You didn't answer my question."

"You didn't ask one."

He resisted rolling his eyes. "Why are you going home this year?"

She shrugged. "My family and I have a rocky relationship. Mostly because I've flaked on them, a lot. I'm . . . undependable. I wanted to change that." She paused. "If I can."

Max thought of the life she led now, going to school, working hard. "You seem pretty dependable to me."

"Yes, well, thankfully things change. People change."
She hesitated again, and he realized she was weighing how much she wanted to tell him. "I'm not sure my family gets that," she finally said. "I've let them down."

He was sympathetic to that. He'd been a punk-ass teenager himself. If his family judged him off that asshole he'd once been, they wouldn't like him very much either. "Then and now are different," he said. "They'll see that."

She didn't look convinced and he couldn't blame her. Because even *he'd* been judging her off something she'd done in the past. Which made him a first-class jerk.

"You do realize the gas pedal is the narrow one on the right," she said.

He glanced over at her. "Excuse me?"

"You're driving like a granny without her spectacles, and I'm in a time crunch."

He choked out a laugh. "In case you haven't noticed, things are a little dicey out there."

She shrugged, unimpressed. "We've both seen worse."

True enough. But she was also deflecting and trying to change the subject. "You left home hard and fast years ago and never looked back. So I don't get it, Rory. What's your sudden rush?"

She looked away. "It's a long story."

"And?"

"And trust me, we don't have enough time."

Before he could react to that, he saw the blockades ahead. "Shit," he said. "Highway's closed."

The flashing sign said there'd been an accident ahead and to please be patient. Ha. Easy enough for the damn sign to say; it wasn't stuck in a car with a woman he couldn't figure out whether he wanted to strangle or kiss.

"Looks like we've suddenly got plenty of time," he said, wondering if she'd talk to him now, surprised at how much he wanted her to. Because in spite of himself, he was fascinated and drawn to *this* Rory, the sexy, smart, resourceful woman sitting next to him. When she didn't respond, he glanced over at her, startled to find her pale, her eyes suspiciously wet. "What?" he asked, whipping his head around to see what had happened, where the big bad was coming from, but he couldn't see a problem. "What is it?"

She just shook her head and began to rifle through her bag, keeping her face averted.

Tears? What had caused such a strong emotion? Clueless and hating that, Max reached down and pulled out a few napkins he kept shoved into the door pouch for those days when he was chowing down a burger and driving at the same time. "Here," he said, and thrust them at her.

She took them without a word and blew her nose. "Thanks," she finally said. "I, um, had something in my eye."

She was talking to her passenger window. Reaching out, he touched her to get her to turn toward him, finding himself stunned when he connected with the bare skin of her arm and felt a zip of electrical current that wasn't electricity at all, but sheer chemistry. "Rory," he said, hardly recognizing his own voice, it was so low and rough.

She stared at him and then her gaze dropped to his

mouth and he had one thought—ah, hell, he was in trouble. Deep trouble.

The next girl you feel something for, anything at all, you have to go for it, no exceptions . . .

He had laughed at Cass's words, secure in the knowledge there wasn't anyone in his life to feel something for right now. Or at least no one he *wanted* to feel something for.

But that was starting to change, right before his very eyes.

Chapter Four

RORY COULDN'T BELIEVE how difficult it was to stop staring at Max's mouth, or to force herself to lift her gaze to his eyes.

Eyes that were dark. Deep. Unfathomable.

He was waiting on an answer. But there was no way she would admit the truth to him, that she felt compelled to get home with her stepdad's gift for her mom by dawn when they opened presents or she wouldn't be forgiven. "I've changed my mind," she said. "It's not a story I'm willing to tell no matter how much time we have."

"Because it makes you cry?" he asked.

"I wasn't crying," she said. "I don't cry."

He arched a brow her way. "Ever?"

"Ever." She narrowed her eyes. "Why, do you?"

"Sure," he said with an easy shrug of his wide shoulders.

Sure. Like it was the most natural thing in the world

to feel so strongly about something that it made you cry. She let out a low, disbelieving laugh. "When?" she asked. "*When* was the last time you cried?"

Max appeared to give this some serious thought. "When I watched *The Good Dinosaur* with my niece last month," he said. "Bawled like a baby." He smiled. "She did too."

Huh. Maybe he was human after all. "Was it the scene where Disney slayed us all through the heart by killing the dad?" she asked. "Or when Spot showed us how he lost his family?"

"Neither," he said. "It happened when my niece ate my ice cream."

She rolled her eyes and turned back to the window.

"Hey," he said, "it was traumatic."

She snorted. "Do you even know the definition of *traumatic*?"

He slid her a look and then gave his attention back to the road, even though they were at a dead stop. "I do," he said.

"Really? You of the perfect family and college basketball scholarship to Michigan State and—"

His head whipped back to hers, his expression dark and incredulous.

Accusatory.

"You know what that thing with Cindy cost me," he finally said. "And I'm over it, long over it, but you can add it to the list of things we're not discussing. Not that and not your part in it, because back then I had no choice but to believe you were the kind of person willing to hurt whoever you had to in order to win. I can concede that maybe you've changed, but history can't be rewritten."

She stared at him, stunned. Cindy had been a classmate who'd taken great pleasure in being as cruel and horrible to Rory as possible. She'd been popular, a great athlete, a great student, and the daughter of the basketball coach. Every guy in the school had crushed on her and she could've had any one of them.

So of course she'd taken the only guy Rory had ever wanted.

Max.

Cindy had been one of those sweet on the outside, toxic on the inside people who were so scary to Rory. It'd been Cindy who in their junior year had lied to their teacher and gotten Rory suspended for cheating when it had been Cindy who'd cheated. Then she'd stolen Rory's clothes from her locker during PE class and had sneakily taken a pic of Rory in her underwear. Cindy had texted it to everyone in school—from Rory's own phone. Just remembering it had her cheeks heating. Her mom and stepdad had been furious at her for all of it, the supposed cheating and the picture. Rory had been devastated and needing sympathy on that in a very bad way, but instead they'd grounded her because they'd actually believed she'd sent that pic herself.

When someone had begun letting themselves into the coach's office to have sex, Cindy started a rumor that it was Rory, all to deflect blame from herself. After all, it wouldn't look good for the sweet, wonderful, lovable coach's daughter to be caught doing it in daddy's office.

Facing expulsion only a week before finals, Rory had finally resorted to taping Cindy leaving her dad's office with a guy in hand. The guy had been in shadow, but there'd been no doubt, at least to her, that it'd been Max.

Yeah, her bad, but she'd had to prove herself innocent. And besides, no one else had seemed to know it was him so she had no idea why he was so pissed. She would ask him but the truth was that she was embarrassed. *Deeply* embarrassed. She wasn't proud of what she'd done. In her mind, the minute she'd turned the tape into the school proving she hadn't been the one breaking into the coach's office, she'd gone from being The Bullied to The Bullier, and she'd hated herself for that.

So much so that she'd left town.

She'd been planning on leaving for a long time anyway. With her mom remarried and having three new kids, it'd been one less mouth to feed, so she'd taken a bus to San Francisco.

Relatively speaking, she'd been one of the lucky runaways. After an admittedly very rough start, she'd taken a part-time job at South Bark, where Willa had tucked her under her wing, teaching her the business and making her take her GED, and in the process had given her back a life that could so easily have gone wrong.

In any case, she was no longer that same Rory she'd once been. When Max had started working in the same building as her last year, she'd been so nervous he'd want to talk about that time in their lives, the time she'd been so very miserable and unhappy.

She had been so relieved when he hadn't seemed to want to talk at all.

But now she realized they should have. Because he was over there on his side of the truck emitting animosity in waves and insinuating that she'd cost him something big.

Not that he appeared at all interested in enlightening her on what.

Fine. She could read between the lines somewhat and she'd get to the bottom of this in her usual way—on her own. For now, he'd turned off the engine to preserve gas, and now it was cold and quickly getting colder. She pulled a blanket from her bag.

He snorted but when she looked at him, he was staring out the windshield, jaw tight, eyes hard, one hand draped over the wheel, the other fisted on a thigh. She figured he was made of stone but she lifted up one end of her blanket in offer. "Cold?" she asked.

"No."

Sensing the thick tension, Carl whined softly.

Rory reached out to test-touch Max's hand.

Cold.

"Seriously?" she asked him and spread half the blanket over his legs.

He didn't help her but when she was finished, she found him staring at her like she was a puzzle and he was missing half the pieces.

But *she* was the one who didn't understand. And she was done not knowing. "So," she said tentatively. "You didn't take your scholarship?"

He closed his eyes for a beat and shook his head. "Why do you keep saying things like that when you know damn well what happened?"

Okay so no, he hadn't taken the scholarship, and she got a feeling in the pit of her stomach that she'd been the direct cause.

Carl whined again.

"Forget it," Max told him. "I'm not letting you out again."

"Max," she said. "I—"

"Finally." He pointed ahead, where the blockades were being removed.

Max cranked over the engine and rolled his window down when a CHP officer came close.

"Don't know how long we'll have the roads open," the guy told them. "It's looking grim."

"Thanks," Max said. "We'll be careful."

And he was. So careful it felt like they were going backward. Rory looked at her phone.

No reception, which meant she couldn't call her stepdad and warn him she'd be late. It was still snowing, it was tense, there was no one else on the road . . . All that, along with the rhythmic slashing of the windshield wipers and the soft blast of the heater left her feeling exhausted. She closed her eyes.

And then jerked upright when the truck slowed and then came to a stop off the side of the road.

She wasn't sure how much time had passed. The snow had been steadily gathering, over a foot now, she saw with some alarm. They'd pulled up behind a small SUV that was leaning awkwardly due to a blown tire.

"Stay here," Max said.

"What are you doing?" she asked.

He spared her a look as he pulled up his hoodie. "Going to help them out."

He said it like it was his problem the SUV was in trouble. Like he could no more pass another car in need of assistance than he could stop inhaling and exhaling air for his lungs.

"But—" she started. But nothing, because he was already gone. She watched him trudge through the snow, lit by his high beams, toward the other SUV.

Two people got out to greet him, an older couple by the looks of them. They spoke to Max, who nodded. Even smiled. He said something to the older man, patted the woman reassuringly on the arm and . . . went to the back of his truck, probably for tools.

"He's going to say he doesn't need anything from me," she said to Carl. "But we're going to offer to help anyway." She pulled her wet sweater and jacket back on and slid out of the truck, smiling at the couple. She moved toward Max, on his knees in the snow now, wrenching off the bad tire with easy strength and ability.

He could be *such* an ass. But he was also selfless. Kind. Funny. Well, at least with everyone else anyway.

The older woman smiled and shook her head at Rory. "We're so grateful that you stopped. We've been here for an hour with no cell service. We couldn't call for help. Our kids and grandkids will be so worried."

Rory managed a smile around a suddenly tight throat. Would her family be worried? Or would they just assume she'd flaked yet again? "You have a big family?"

"You might say so." The woman laughed. "Six kids.

Twelve grandkids." She laughed again at the look on Rory's face. "We've been together since the dawn of time, you see." She looked toward the men, shaking hands now since Max was already finished, and beamed. "And after all these years, he still makes my heart flutter."

"That's incredibly sweet," Rory said.

The older woman squeezed her hand. "Whatever you two are arguing about, my dear, you can work it out."

Rory looked at her, startled. "How do you know we're arguing?"

"Since the dawn of time, remember? I know the signs." She smiled. "Would you like a hint on how to fix it?"

Rory looked into her kind eyes. "Yes, please."

"You use the past to fix the now," she said. "You make your mistakes—which is allowed, by the way. After all, you're only human, but you learn from them. Grow from them. Things can't always be forgotten, but they can be forgiven."

Rory turned to look at Max. She'd most definitely learned from her mistakes. Grown from them. But . . . had she been forgiven for them?

The old couple got into their SUV and drove off. Rory helped Max gather the few tools he'd used.

"Get in the truck," he said. "I've got this."

She stubbornly went to the back of the truck with him to put the tools away. They both leaned in, reaching out to close the toolbox at the same time, their faces close, their hands colliding. She took in the scent of him, some sort of innately sexy guy soap. He hadn't shaved that morning and the sight of the stubble on his strong jaw had a funny slide going through her belly.

Suddenly he appeared to realize how close their faces were and jerked back. "Get out of the snow," he said.

He was just as covered in it as she. In fact, every inch of his jacket was layered in fresh powder. "Right back at you," she said.

Reaching out, he ran a hand over her head and shoulders, brushing snow from her, an action that had the quiver in her belly heading south.

She didn't want to feel anything for him, she really didn't, but she couldn't seem to stop herself. A low sound that came horrifying close to a moan escaped her and Max stilled.

God. He'd heard and now her humiliation was complete—

"Get in the truck and out of this weather," he repeated, his voice still low and rough but somehow softer. "*Please.*"

She drew in a surprised breath at that. She wasn't used to the "please," not from him anyway. She nodded and left him alone.

Two minutes later he'd joined her and Carl in the truck and . . .

The engine wouldn't start.

Chapter Five

"SHIT," MAX SAID after a few more tries. He leaned back, frustration in every line of his body.

"What's wrong?" Rory asked, afraid she already knew.

"Dead battery." He shook his head. "I was going to give the truck an overhaul this week with my dad and that's one of the things I was going to replace. I think the frigid temps finished her off."

Rory looked at the time. Eleven thirty. On Christmas Eve, no less. Not good, not good at all, but she tried not to panic.

And failed miserably.

"So . . . what now?" she asked in what she hoped was a casual voice.

He glanced over at her as if maybe she'd given away her panic regardless. He pulled out his phone and looked at the screen. "Still no cell service," he said in disgust. "I'm going to have to flag someone down for a jump-start."

She had no idea how long that would take but it surely wasn't going to be quick and her heart sank. Getting home by dawn wasn't looking good, but surely *someone* would stop. She looked out into the night.

Not another vehicle in sight.

It was like they were on Mars.

Use the past to fix the now . . . The woman's words floated around in her head and it came to her that maybe this trip could be about more than just making up with her family. She could make up with Max. If he'd let her. "Max?"

"Yeah?"

"Did Cindy break up with you after I turned in the video?" she asked. "Is that why you're mad at me?"

Max leaned forward and knocked his head against his steering wheel several times.

"Look," she said softly. "I'm sorry. And I should've said that a long time ago. The video . . . it wasn't about you—"

Head still down, he snorted.

"It wasn't," she insisted.

Max shook his head, straightened, and slid out of the truck.

No doubt to get away from her.

Standing there in the glare of the headlights, legs spread, feet solidly planted against the wind and snow, he looked tough as hell.

But so was she, she reminded herself.

So she got out and stood next to him.

"What are you doing?" He had to raise his voice to be heard over the wind. "Get back inside."

She couldn't. She had to know; it was killing her. "What did I cost you, Max?"

He shoved his hands into his pockets. He was watching the highway, clearly willing a car to come along that he could flag down. But there was no one but her.

"Max, please," she said. "Just tell me."

He inhaled deeply. "Cindy got suspended," he said. "A hand slap, considering. They didn't know it was me in the tape but I had to—" He shook his head. "We'd already moved on from each other but I still couldn't not say anything . . ."

She wasn't going to like this story, she could tell. "You came forward," she guessed.

He shrugged, like there'd been no other option.

How had she not seen that coming? No way would a guy like Max let a girl take all the blame for something he'd been involved in as well.

"And then I was suspended too," he said.

"Oh, Max," she breathed. "I'm so sorry."

He turned to her then, his eyes hard. "It wasn't the suspension that got me. Hell, I deserved it. I did it. I was there and I knew we shouldn't be and I'm just lucky I wasn't expelled. But Coach . . . he was royally pissed off and looking for blood. He cut me from the team for misconduct, which broke the verbal contract I had to go play for Michigan State. They dumped me."

She stared at him in horror. "But you were so good," she said. "Why didn't someone else pick you up?"

"Most teams were already full. After I graduated, I could've walked on somewhere and tried out, but we couldn't afford for me to go anywhere without a guaranteed scholarship. So I didn't."

She told herself it was the wind and icy cold stinging her eyes. "Max, I—"

"If you're about to say you're sorry, save it."

"But—"

"Someone's coming," he said, eyes sharp on the road. "Get back in the truck—"

"Max—"

"Dammit, Rory, this isn't exactly safe, okay? We're out on the highway, fairly defenseless. I want you locked in the truck until I see who stops for us."

Okay, she got that, but she hated the idea of him being out here on his own.

He laughed a little harshly, as if reading her thoughts. "I might not have ended up with a degree but trust me, princess, I'm qualified for this."

"Call me princess one more time and I'll—"

"*Truck*," he said tightly.

Getting that she was a liability at the moment, she did as he'd asked and got into the truck.

Which was when she realized it was empty of one oversized Doberman. "Carl?"

Nothing.

Where the hell had he gone? Realizing he must have escaped when she'd gotten out, she whirled back around to get her eyes on Max. She watched him step closer to the approaching car but not too close, bending down a little to peek into the passenger window when it slid down only a few inches.

He looked like quite the imposing figure, tall, built, fiercely serious in the moment, and she wondered what they were talking about.

Then he turned his head and looked right at her through the windshield and she knew. They were talking about her.

Max nodded to the person in the car and then he strode through the driving snow toward her.

"Max," she said immediately when he came around, not to the driver's side but to her passenger side and opened the door. "Carl's gone."

He stood there in the vee of space between the door and the body of the truck, sheltering her from the worst of the storm. "He probably went into the woods to do his business. He'll be right back. About the car—"

"Are they going to help?" she asked.

"It's a guy in a big hurry to get to his wife," he said. "She's in labor at the hospital in Tahoe. He promised to call for a tow truck as soon as he got over the summit and got any reception."

"Do you think he will?"

Max shrugged. "I hope so. I know him, or I know who he is. He works with my older sister at the post office. He's a good guy, married with three other kids. He says you can hitch a ride with him so you won't miss Christmas morning. But you have to decide right this minute. He's out of time."

If she went, she could get home by dawn and make amends with her family. It was perfect and she was grateful for the offer but—

Max, apparently taking her silence as a yes, reached in to take her hand.

"No," she said, resisting but not letting go of his hand. Her heart was pounding. She knew she should take this opportunity and go. That's what this whole thing was all about—getting home in time. Or that's what she thought it'd been all about.

But in that moment, she knew it was about far more. Like being a better person, one who put others first.

"No?" he repeated.

"No. Thank you but no. I'm not going when you're stranded here with Carl missing."

"I'll find Carl," he said.

"You might need help," she insisted. "I'm not leaving you."

He stared at her in disbelief. "Rory, I can handle this."

"Maybe." Okay, definitely. Not the point. She wasn't walking away from a friend. And yeah, maybe at the moment they weren't friends exactly, but they were . . . *something*. "I'm still not leaving you out here alone in this storm on the side of the road," she said. "So tell him thank you and good luck to him and his wife but I'm staying with you."

Max looked at her as if she'd lost her damn mind but he strode back to the car, said a few words, and then the car was gone, leaving them alone on top of the world in a massive blizzard.

Max whistled for Carl but the wind was so loud, the sound got swallowed up.

Rory slipped out of the truck and back into the mind

numbing cold to make her way to Max. "Carl!" she yelled and nearly got blown over by the next gust of wind.

Max caught her and held her at his side. "You could've gotten home," he said. "You know you're crazy, right?" he asked.

Yes, she knew. And yeah, her whole purpose had been to show her family she'd changed but hey, there'd be plenty of time to stress about that later. "This is for Carl, not you."

He choked out a rough laugh. "You're still crazy," he said but he'd kept his arm around her, holding her close. And he didn't sound quite as mad at her anymore.

Which might have just been wishful thinking on her part.

"Carl!" Max yelled, using the hand that wasn't holding onto her to cup around his mouth. "Carl, *come!*"

From out of the woods came a huge snow abomination. When it was only a few feet from them, it stopped, shook, and sent snow flying.

Carl.

Proud of himself, he sat happily at their feet and panted a smile, while Rory fought with relieved tears.

What was wrong with her tonight?

Max got them all back into the truck. He dried off Carl the best he could and then turned to Rory.

She had no idea that she'd lost the battle with her emotions until Max cupped her face and swiped a tear from her cheek with his thumb. "Rory," he said, voice low and concerned.

"Does Christmas always have to suck so hard?" she whispered.

He looked at her for a long beat and then slowly shook his head. "No. Not always."

They stared at each other some more and then . . . he kissed her. Softly at first, carefully, but she didn't need either and let him know by fisting her hands in his jacket and letting out a needy little whimper for more.

This wrenched a deep, rough male groan from him that rumbled up from his chest, and she clutched at him, trying to get closer. Before she knew it, he'd hauled her over the console and into his lap, tucking her thighs on either side of his, letting her feel *exactly* how his body had responded to the kiss. He was hard.

Everywhere.

Hungry for the connection, desperate to forget her problems, trembling in her boots for more of this man beneath her, she kissed him back with all the pent-up longing and need she felt. When they broke free, his eyes were heavy-lidded with lust and desire, and she had one single, devastating thought.

All these years later, she still wanted him as her own.

Chapter Six

MAX DIDN'T OFTEN act without deliberate conscious thought. In his job, his life depended on him being a clear, levelheaded thinker at all times.

But at the moment, with the wind and snow beating up his truck on the outside, the interior both dark and intimate, his tongue halfway down Rory's throat, he couldn't kick-start his brain or mobilize his thoughts. All he could do was feel. And, Christ, what he felt. Rory's loose hair streaming over his shoulders and arms as she strained against him, her petite body chilled enough to sink in and concern him—which was an excuse to wrap her up even tighter in his arms.

Better.

Carl gave a happy "wuff," and clearly thinking they were *all* going to wrestle, he tried to stick his big, fat head in between them.

Rory choked out a laugh and gave the dog a playful

shove and then, in what might have been Max's favorite part of the day, hell his entire year, Rory slid her fingers back into his hair and kissed *him*.

Yeah, that worked. Big time. He tried to keep it light but she kept responding with more than he expected, sweeping her tongue into his mouth, sliding it sensually against his, and he was a goner. With a groan, he tightened his grip on her and gave her all he had.

She whispered his name, her voice filled with such longing that it reached deep inside his chest and squeezed around his heart. She was still straddling him, her knees tucked on either side of his hips, and then she rocked against his killer hard-on and he forgot to breathe. But breathing was optional anyway as he kissed her hungrily, completely lost in her, just gone.

When she finally pulled free, she was breathless, her eyes dazed, her lips full and wet. "What was that for?" she asked softly.

He had no idea. She was driving him crazy. Since the day he'd begun working in the same building as her and he'd realized that there was a serious chemistry between them, she'd been driving him crazy. But this was a whole new level of crazy, the kind that made him want to get her naked so he could warm her up in the most basic of ways.

Not good.

None of this was good, this seeing new sides of her that he didn't want to see. Rory sharing everything she had, Rory being sweet and kind. Resourceful. And incredibly courageous. And, Christ, but he really loved that about her. She'd been through hell and was here on the other side, stronger than ever.

The thing was, in his life, he took care of people. Clients at work. Coworkers. Carl. His friends. His family. Although . . . it hadn't escaped him who'd been taking care of who on this trip.

"Max?"

"I don't know what that was," he said. "You turn me upside down."

She let out a snort. Clearly he wasn't the only one off his axis.

Headlights came up behind them, uncomfortably close. All he could see in the dark night was that the vehicle was large. Possibly a tow truck, *hopefully* a tow truck but possibly not, and he carefully nudged Rory off his lap and back to her seat. Her eyes widened when he leaned forward to grab the Maglite he'd left at his feet and his jacket raised up, clearly revealing the gun at the small of his back.

"What—"

"Wait here," he said, and then he slid out of the truck, locking it behind him. They were on a deserted road in a damn blizzard.

Sitting ducks.

But it was a tow truck. "Got a call," the driver said, hopping out. "Bad battery?"

"Yeah, if you can just give me a jump, I should be able to get it home and replace it."

The guy nodded and they went to work.

"Hopefully you get all the way through," the tow truck

driver said when they had Max's truck running again. "I heard they're going to close the road five miles up. There's a wreck that they might not get cleared until morning."

Hell. "Thanks." He got back into his truck and looked at Rory. And Carl too, since he was once again in her lap, the big baby. Max didn't feel like smiling but that's exactly what he did since his dog was bigger than she was. "Shouldn't *you* be in *his* lap?"

She had her arms wrapped around Carl in a hug and they looked pretty comfy. "He wanted a snuggle."

No shit. Any male in his right mind would want a snuggle from Rory. The thought surprised him. But it was the utter truth. "We can go back," he said, "or we can forge forward with no guarantee. What's your vote?"

She looked surprised. "You're giving me a say?"

"Yes," he said. "Merry Christmas."

She rolled her eyes but stared at him some more, her expression going solemn and serious. Whatever her thoughts, they were deep and troubled, and he knew it was related to why she was in such a desperate hurry to get home.

"I vote forge forward," she finally said.

He nodded. "Forward it is then."

But three minutes later he was second-guessing their decision. The snow had gotten worse and so had the driving conditions.

"I get why you're mad at me," Rory said quietly. "And I know it won't help anything, but . . . "

"I don't need an apology from you," he said. He felt her gaze on him but kept his on the road. "*Shit.*"

"What?"

He pointed to the flashing sign ahead: *Highway closed three miles ahead.*

Take next exit to turn around.

She didn't speak, but her sucked in gasp spoke volumes. They were silent as he got off at the exit. They were in a very small mountain town. Actually *town* might be a bit overstated. There was a gas station, a convenience store, and a tiny motel. Emphasis on *tiny*.

Max pulled into the lot. "I'm going to ask you one more time—go back or stay and get rooms?"

She bit her lower lip.

"It's one in the morning," he said. "I'm exhausted. You look exhausted."

Carl let out a low huff.

"And Carl's exhausted," he added and got a ghost of a smile from Rory. "If we get rooms, we would get some sleep and hopefully the roads will open up at daylight."

"Daylight," she repeated softly, staring out the window. "So we won't make it home by dawn."

There was something in her voice. Emotion. Deep emotion. "Better than going back to San Francisco though, right?" he asked.

She didn't answer.

"Rory? Stay or go?"

She closed her eyes. "Stay."

"Okay." He nodded. "Do you want to call home? I'm sure there's a phone in there we can use."

"It's too late," she said softly. "They go to bed early. It's okay, I'll call them in the morning. I don't want to walk up the whole house."

"Okay. Wait here with Carl for a sec, I've gotta go try to bribe them into letting him stay as well, otherwise I'm stuck in the truck."

"*We're* stuck in the truck," she said, reaching to pet Carl.

We. Shit. He hoped to God he had enough cash on him to bribe whoever was in that motel, because the close quarters inside the truck would kill him long before dawn.

Chapter Seven

MAX DIDN'T WAIT for an answer; he just slid out of the truck and strode purposefully toward the small motel. Rory watched him go, his gait confident, those broad shoulders squared against the wind.

"He never second-guesses himself, does he?" she murmured to Carl, her own shoulders slumping.

Carl, who'd climbed into the driver's seat the second Max had vacated it, licked her chin.

"He's also still not thrilled with me, kiss or no," she said.

Carl whined and sniffed at her bag, probably hungry for another PB&J.

"At least it finally makes sense now, given what I cost him." She sighed. "I really blew it, Carl."

He whined again and bumped his face to hers. She hugged him tight, burying her face in the short but soft fur at his neck. "I knew you'd forgive me."

Back then she'd really believed turning in the video had been a victory. Her first. She'd actually won at something, gotten the upper hand.

But she'd been wrong. It'd been a terribly selfish thing to do, leaving Max to pay the price, and what was worse, she hadn't even realized it because she'd been blinded by her need for revenge.

She really hated that.

She startled when Max opened the door and wind and snow blew in. "Let's go," he said.

"They'll take Carl?"

"Had to pay double, but yeah." He grabbed their two bags and tossed her the leash. "You got him?"

For some reason that made her feel slightly better. Though he had good reason to hate her, he didn't, not if he trusted her with Carl. Maybe he'd finally really hear her apology. "Max?"

He turned to her, impatience on his face. There were snowflakes clinging to his perfectly long, inky black eyelashes, and his jaw was tight.

She bit her lower lip. "I just want to say how sorry I am that—"

"Not now."

"Then when?"

His laugh was humorless. "Rory, it's ten fucking degrees and it's coming down sideways out here. You're shaking so hard your teeth are going to rattle out of your mouth."

"I don't care." She reached out and grabbed a fistful of his jacket to hold him still. "I'm trying to make everything okay, Max. Don't you get it? I really *need* everything to be okay. God, just once in my life, I need that. I can't live with all this past stuff in my head anymore, I'm going to lose my mind." She gripped his jacket tighter and put her face in his. "So I'm going to tell you I'm sorry and you're going to listen to me, dammit!"

He hadn't so much as blinked as she basically yelled at him but she thought maybe there was the slightest softening in his hard eyes. "Okay," he said.

"Okay." She let out a breath and nodded. "Good."

"You ready to go inside now or do you need to yell at me some more?" he asked.

She choked out a laugh and got out of the truck.

The lobby of the motel consisted of a desk and a love seat that looked like it'd seen better days. So did the paint on the walls and the floors. The wide-screen TV though, that was brand spanking new and the twentysomething guy in front of it waved them through a hallway without taking his eyes off his show. "Last two rooms on the right," he said, glancing over, his gaze slowing a little as he took in Rory. "They connect if you want them to," he added slyly.

Rory stumbled but Max caught her and nudged her along without comment.

To their connecting rooms.

She didn't say a word as they stopped in front of the first door. Max handed her a key and waited until she unlocked it.

"Try to get some sleep," he said. "I'll come for you when the roads are open and clear."

"You kissed me."

"Yeah."

"You kissed me like you *liked* me," she said.

He just held her gaze as snow flew all around them.

She drew a deep breath. "Max, the girl who made that video, she isn't the same woman standing here in front of you. You have to know that."

Max dropped his head and stared at his boots for a beat before meeting her gaze again. "Look, maybe we could go in our rooms and take showers to recover from the snow apocalypse, and then take some time to think things through like rational people. Would that work for you?"

She paused and then nodded.

A very slight bit of humor came into his gaze. "You sure?" he asked. "Because if you want to go back outside in this crazy-ass storm and yell at me on Christmas Eve some more, that works too."

She rolled her eyes and turned back to her door. "The rooms connect."

"Yes."

She glanced at him. "You going to knock first?"

He studied her for a long moment and then stepped into her a little bit, enough to make her breathing hitch and her heart skip a beat. His fingers stroked a rogue strand of hair from her temple. "Worried?"

Yes. She was worried that he *wouldn't* come over at all.

"Listen," he said. "Let it all go for tonight, okay? I mean what's the worst that could happen—you wake up and go back to worrying in the morning? Because maybe life'll surprise you and everything'll be fine."

She gave a rough laugh and he smiled. "It could happen," he said.

"Not in my world."

His smile faded. "There's a first time for everything, Rory. Shut and lock the door. You know where to find me if you need me."

He said this lightly but she had a feeling he was hoping she wouldn't need him. Which was fine. She didn't need anyone, thank you very much. So she did as he said. She shut and locked her door and stared at the small but neat room. She set down her duffle bag and then eyeballed the connecting door to Max's room.

The walls were thin. She could hear him unlocking his door and then the padding of Carl as he trotted in.

"Stop," Max said and Rory froze.

"Don't drool on the windows."

Rory had to laugh at herself and then imagined Carl at the window, up on his back legs so he could see out into the night.

"You wouldn't believe the security deposit I had to put down for you," Max said, tone warning, "and I want it back, every penny."

There was a thump. Probably Max's duffle bag hitting the floor. And then the interior door, her connecting door, rattled a tiny bit.

He'd unlocked his connecting door, she realized as her heart took a good solid leap.

He wanted her to be able to get him if she needed him.

"Don't even think about the bed," Max said. "I've got

dibs. I'm taking a quick shower first. Don't eat anything while I'm gone, you hear me?"

There was a silence and then the sound of a door shutting and water coming on.

Max in the shower.

A thought that gave Rory a hot flash. The guy went to the gym. He ran. He kicked ass at work. He was all solid, lean muscle, and knowing he was stripping down and stepping into a steamy hot shower had her pulse rate in overdrive.

She tried to remind herself that he didn't like her very much but she had to admit, his actions toward her didn't support that theory. He'd given her a ride. He'd looked out for her, finding her an alternate ride when his truck had failed them. He'd gotten her a motel room. He'd been protective, if not exactly the "gentle" that Willa had asked him for, and he'd certainly been kind.

And then there'd been the kiss that had led to a make-out session for the record books. Just thinking about it had her nipples hard again and started that tingle in her thighs.

She liked him, she *really* liked him.

And she always had.

"Dammit," she whispered.

Get some sleep, he'd said. But she knew she wouldn't. She couldn't.

She'd cost him a scholarship.

She'd ruined his life.

No, she wouldn't sleep. Not until she knew she'd done her best to make things right.

Chapter Eight

MAX STOOD IN the shower, hands flat on the tile wall, his head bent so that the hot water could beat down on him.

My family and I have a rocky relationship. I've flaked on them, a lot. I'm . . . undependable. I wanted to change that this year. . .

It pissed him off that Rory's family didn't see her for the incredible woman she was. She deserved support from them. Shaking his head, he turned off the water and grabbed a towel.

I'm still not leaving you out here alone in this storm on the side of the road . . .

He still couldn't believe how amazingly fierce she'd been, standing there in the crazy storm, teeth chattering and still, refusing to leave him alone.

Not the sign of a flaky woman, one who didn't care about anyone other than herself. In fact, she was the exact opposite of that.

Running the towel over his wet head, he stepped out of the bathroom and heard a sharp gasp.

Definitely not Carl.

Lifting his head, he met Rory's shocked gaze as it ran down the length of his nude body.

"Um," she said.

He arched a brow. "Didn't hear you knock."

"Um," she said again but didn't, he couldn't help but notice, look away.

He walked to the duffle bag on the floor, squatted low, and rifled through for a clean pair of jeans. Straightening, he pulled them on and turned back to her.

She blinked. "You're . . . commando."

"And you found your words again."

She rolled her eyes so hard he was surprised they didn't come out of the sockets. "I'm just discombobulated because we didn't get home," she said just defensively enough to make him grin.

"And here I thought it was me naked."

"Fine," she said, blushing. "Maybe it was a little bit you naked."

"Yeah, if you could not use 'little' and 'naked' in the same sentence about me," he said and smiled when she found a laugh.

"Okay, I want to start over." She took a deep breath. "I cost you your college education."

He shook his head. "I shouldn't have told you that."

"Yes, you should have. I still can't believe I didn't know." She shook her head, looking devastated. "No wonder you hated me all this time, and now you're stuck with me on Christmas Eve and I don't even have a present to give you in the morning."

He choked out a low laugh. "I never hated you, Rory."

A lot crossed her face at that. Hope. Relief. "No?"

"No." He hesitated, something he rarely did. "Look, if we're sharing and all that, then there's some things you should know."

Her gaze locked on his and held. "Like?"

He sighed. "It's true that back then I was pissed off. I was angry at the world, actually, and also going out with girls I wouldn't look twice at now because I was a first-class ass, but I'm glad it all happened the way it did. I wouldn't change it."

"You wouldn't?" she asked, her fingers tightly entwined together, knuckles white.

Shaking his head, he stepped toward her and took her hands in his, gently applying pressure until she loosened her fingers so he could clasp them in his. "I'd have ended up in Michigan," he said. "It's fucking cold in Michigan."

She snorted. "It's fucking cold *here*."

He smiled and shook his head. "Not in this room it's not."

She caught her lower lip between her teeth. "Max—"

"My point is that I love San Francisco," he said. "I love my job, my place, my friends. My life there is good. Great, actually."

She let out a long, shaky breath. "Thanks. You didn't have to say that."

"Yeah," he said, letting his hands come up to her arms. "I did."

She met his gaze, her own honest and earnest and re-morseful. "I really am so very sorry. What I did was selfish, and worse, I never even gave a second thought to the mess I left you in. It was all about me trying to get revenge on Cindy, but you got screwed over so much more than she did."

True. He'd been dumped by his very angry coach, hu-miliated in front of the entire town, and his family had been shocked and disappointed in him. He hadn't gotten over it for a damn long time, certainly much longer than anyone cared about the damn video. And he'd been con-fused too, because he'd liked Rory. She'd been quiet but nice. And funny. He'd never seen her as one of the mean girls. "Why did you do it?" he asked. "What did you mean, you wanted revenge on Cindy?"

She gave him a questioning look. "You knew that she accused me of being the one to break into her dad's office. She said that she'd seen me do it, that I was the one steal-ing money from the coaches' bags, among other things."

"No," Max said slowly. "I didn't know that."

"When I actually caught her at it, she turned it around on me," she said softly, her eyes on his. "I was suspended."

"I knew you'd been suspended for stealing something from the school but I didn't know what."

She shook her head. "I didn't steal anything. And she kept getting me in trouble, one thing after another, making things up so I came off as unreliable in case I tried to turn her in."

"I'm sorry," he said. "I'd like to say I dumped her for being a bitch but the fact is, I didn't care what she was like. You should have turned her in regardless."

She just looked at him.

"Oh." He let out a low laugh. "Right. You did. You videoed her and got me as well."

"A mistake," she said. "You were collateral damage, and I'm so very sorry, Max."

He got that. He appreciated that. But the past was the past and he had some things to say too. "Listen, I was a teenage jerk and I thought the world revolved around me. It never occurred to me that you were in trouble, that you weren't even targeting me. I was *that* self-absorbed, and I hate that."

She started to shake her head and say something more but he covered her lips with a finger. He needed to finish, to get this out, because he was realizing a couple of things. He'd wronged her in much the same way everyone else in her life had, and that was a hard pill to swallow because he prided himself on always trying to do the right thing. "You're done apologizing to me," he said. "I was a complete dick about it earlier, but I was wrong. Then and now."

"Max—"

He applied gentle pressure on her mouth. "There's nothing to forgive, okay? You were only doing what you had to to get through and I get it. Now it's my turn to apologize to you."

This startled her into silence. He smiled, his fingers stroking her jaw while his thumb rasped over her lower lip. "I should have listened to you. But also I should've known there was more to the story. I should've asked you, but maybe it's better that we waited because we're old now and . . . " He stopped to smile when she choked out a laugh. "And with all this dubious maturing I've realized something."

She sucked in a breath and lifted her worried gaze to his. "What?"

With a slight shake of his head, he bent a little and brushed his mouth over hers. "There's something I want."

"Another kiss?" she asked, her voice a hopeful whisper that made his chest both swell and ache at the same time.

"Yes," he said. "But more."

"A bunch of kisses?"

At the hint of laughter in her voice, he smiled. She'd relaxed and was teasing him. "More," he said softly.

She blinked. "You . . . want to sleep with me?"

"Oh yes," he breathed, pulling her in. "I want that, Rory. And I want it bad too. But still more."

"I . . . don't understand."

"I want something between us."

She froze. "Like . . . a condom?"

He laughed and pressed his forehead to hers. He kept thinking about what his sister said, about him giving the next woman he felt something for a shot. A real shot. He really hated to ever admit Cass might have been onto something, but he honestly had never felt this way about another woman before. "A relationship," he said and watched her mouth fall open.

"I— You—" She gulped in air. "With me?"

Now they were on the same page. A damn long time coming too. "Yes," he said and kissed her, liking the way she melted into him as if her body was way ahead of her brain at this point. "You in?"

She stared up at him. "I'm not very good at relation-ships," she said very seriously.

"Says who?"

This seemed to stymie her. "Every guy I've ever dated?"

"Then you've been dating the wrong guys." He rubbed his jaw to hers. "Take a chance, Rory. Take the risk."

Her hands came up to his face, her fingers slipping into his hair, and it felt so good he tightened his grip on her.

"I've got a bad track record with the people in my life," she said quietly and shook her head when he started to speak. "No, you know it's true. I'm not a good bet, Max. In fact, I'm a really bad one."

That she absolutely believed this broke his heart. She'd survived a shitty childhood and then a rough stint on her own in San Francisco. But she *had* survived, even thrived. And then there was how she'd handled tonight and all the storm had thrown at them without blinking an eye.

And yet this, with him—which should've been one of the easier things in her life—scared the hell out of her.

"You need to believe me on this," she said, backing free of him. "I'm not built that way, I'm not good at rela-tionships. I'm not good at letting people in and keeping them. I don't know how."

He caught her and reeled her panicking body in. "It's okay," he said very gently, cupping her face, tilting it to his to make sure she heard him. "Because I do."

While she continued to stare up at him, he lowered his head and gave her a soft kiss. And then a not-so-soft kiss that he seemed to have trouble tearing himself free of. "You have no idea, do you," he murmured, "why I bring Carl in every week to get groomed. And it's not because he needs it. It's because we've both got it bad for you. We use all available opportunities as an excuse to see you."

She choked out a surprised laugh. "That is a costly way to do it."

He laughed. "I know. Do you trust me, Rory?"

"Yes," she said without a beat of hesitation.

"I wanted to drive you here," he said. "I wanted any reason at all to spend time with you. I'm serious about you, and if I'm being honest, that's been building for a long time."

He could tell by the look on her face that she was serious about him too, scared to death or not.

"I think about you," he told her.

She shook her head. "When? When do you think about me?"

"When I'm sleeping. And working. And not working." He stopped to take in her smile. "You're the one for me, Rory. And I think you feel the same way about me."

She could've lied her way out of that if she wanted. He knew she had the skills. But she didn't. Holding his gaze in hers, she backed him to the bed and then, still holding eye contact, gave him a shove to his chest that had him dropping to the mattress.

He laughed but that laughter stuck in his throat when she got on the bed and slowly climbed up his body, letting him feel her, all of her, and with a groan he began to wrap her up tight in her arms and—

That's when they were jumped by 150 pounds of dog wanting to get in on the fun, panting dog breath in their faces, making Rory laugh.

Max loved the sound and smiled at her as he reared up to kiss her, having to reach around Carl, but Rory stopped him with a hand to his chest.

He stilled. "Problem?" he asked. "Other than the heavyweight road block named Carl?"

At the sound of his name, Carl barked, excited they were finally having all the fun.

"I think maybe he's trying to tell us something," Rory said.

"Like?"

"Like . . . like maybe we're moving too fast."

"I don't think Carl's that deep of a thinker," he said. "Down."

Rory started to shift but he gripped her and with a laugh said, "Carl. *Carl*, down. You stay."

Carl promptly rolled onto his back on the bed, taking up nearly the entire thing and showing off all his bits as he did.

"Well, you did say down," Rory pointed out. "He listens. He laid down. What a good boy," she said to his dog. "Are you a good boy, Carl?"

Carl's tail thumped the bed staccato style.

Max pointed to the floor.

Carl hefted out a sigh and slunk off the mattress. Slowly. One long leg at a time, with a look back at Max as each limb hit the floor like he was hoping he'd change his mind.

Max didn't. Instead, he tucked Rory beneath him, entwined his fingers in hers, and slowly slid their hands over her head as he lowered his.

"So," he said. "Where were we?"

Chapter Nine

RORY STARED UP at Max, mesmerized by the warm look in his eyes. "I think you were about to rock my world," she whispered.

He smiled. "Was I?"

Her heart sped up. God, he had a gorgeous smile. "I hope so," she said fervently.

He pulled her sweater slowly over her head. It fell to the floor and she heard him suck in a breath, which was reassuring in a sexy, "ohmigod this is happening" way because it meant she did it for him every bit as much as he did it for her.

Pressing herself up against the long, leanly muscled body she'd been dreaming about for ages, she wrapped her arms around him and pressed her face into his throat. He smelled amazing and, needing to know if he tasted amazing as well, she took a little nibble.

He growled low in his throat at that and tipped her chin up. "Tell me you're in this, Rory."

If she was any more in, she'd be drowning. "I'm in this."

He stared into her eyes for a beat as if searching for the truth in that statement, but she'd never been so honest with anyone in her life. "I want you, Max. I always have."

That had a fierce light blazing from his intense eyes and then he claimed her mouth. She loved that he wasn't gentle with her. She didn't need or want that, and she moaned when he kissed her hard and hot and hungry all at once. And then he was busy divesting her of the rest of her clothing until she was bared to him. With a shaky breath he took her in, and when that made her shift uncomfortably, he caught her hands and bent to press his mouth to the throbbing pulse at the base of her neck, slowly working his way south.

"Soft," he murmured. "So soft. Sweet too."

She managed a laugh.

He lifted his head, eyes crinkled in amusement. "What?"

"No one's ever called me sweet before."

"Well, you do hide it well," he said demurely, making her snort. He flicked a tongue across her nipple and then sucked it into his mouth, leaving her a trembling wreck. He moved south then, taking his sweet-ass time too, nipping her just beneath her belly button, her hip. "You'll stop me if there's anything you don't like," he said.

"At the moment, I'm more likely to beg you to keep going."

He smiled. "Like the sound of that too." His big hands urged her legs to part, and he lowered his head and rubbed his stubbly jaw against her inner thigh while she squirmed and wriggled.

He simply tightened his grip on her, holding her still while he turned his head and worked her other inner thigh, and then finally, finally he found a new target, the perfect spot, her holy grail spot . . . without so much as a road map or directions.

Before she could marvel over this, she was gone. Lost in wave after wave of sensation that robbed her of her senses while she burst apart at the seams.

When she surfaced back to reality, he'd located a condom from she had no idea where, but she was grateful. "Yes," she said. *"Please, yes."*

His gaze riveted on hers, his mouth curved as he kissed her. "Love the 'please,'" he murmured, voice sexy, low and rough. "Feel free to give me more of that."

She was laughing as he slid home but the laughter backed up in her throat, turning into a moan. Helplessly she arched into him, filled to bursting as he claimed her mouth again.

And then he began to move and claimed her body as well, taking her to a place she'd never been before. When they both fell apart, shuddering in each other's arms, Rory couldn't catch her breath, couldn't get it together.

She didn't have to. He held her for a long time after, rolling onto his back, taking her with him so that she was plastered all over him, a tangle of limbs. His arms remained tight around her, one hand gliding slowly up and down her back, occasionally stopping to squeeze her ass.

It made her smile and her heart sigh. She fell asleep like that, more content then she could ever remember feeling, thinking if only Christmas could end right here, it'd be perfect.

RORY OPENED HER eyes to find Max standing over her with a steaming cup in his hand and a sexy, knowing smile on his face.

He'd spent the past few hours rocking her world and he damn well knew it. It'd been . . . amazing, but now she was short of sleep and felt like roadkill. Probably looked like it too.

But not Max. Nope, he had the nerve to look reenergized and perfect.

With a groan, Rory rolled over and planted her face in the pillow.

"Mmm," he murmured huskily in her ear, clearly taking her new position as an invitation. "Later, if you're really, really good." And then he lightly smacked her ass. "Rise and shine, princess."

She gave him a kick but missed by a mile because he had reflexes like a cat.

He merely laughed and set the steaming cup by the bed. "A real morning person, I see."

"Anyone ever tell you that you're more fun when you're not talking?" she muttered, muffled by the pillow.

He laughed again, telling her that he *was* a morning person, which meant she might have to kill him.

"We've gotta go," he said.

With a gasp, she sat right up, clutching the sheet to her chest. "It's morning?"

"Almost. But I wanted to talk to you before we go."

Oh boy. A talk. In her experience, nothing good ever came out of a talk, and she flopped back into her face-down position.

His hand was on her ass again, squeezing now. "Of course, there're other ways to get your attention . . . "

Not before she at least brushed her teeth, there wasn't. She rolled onto her back to tell him so but he was there, right there, leaning over her, easily taking control of the sheet, tugging it southward.

"Okay, okay, I'm listening!" she claimed, tightening her tenuous grip on it.

But the sheet still slid south, with Max watching from warm, sexy, hooded eyes as she was revealed to him inch by inch until the sheet rested just below her hips.

Leaving her bare-ass naked on the bed.

With a squeak, she reached for the covers, but with a grin, he held them out of her reach, heavy sexual intent in his gaze.

Carl, mistaking the commotion as fun time, jumped up with a bark.

"Sorry, buddy," Max said. "She's all mine."

The words should've annoyed the hell out of Rory; instead they gave her a hot rush. *All his . . .*

Nudging the dog aside and dropping the sheet onto the floor, Max snatched Rory and pulled her in.

He was dressed. He smelled fresh and clean and his hair was wet.

The day had started without her.

"I don't do talks while naked," she managed, once again trying to reach for the covers.

Max leaned in a little further, taking hold of her wrists, sliding them up the bed, alongside of her head. "Let me offer an incentive." He kissed her, starting with the lightest brush of lips against hers but working up both the pressure and the heat. When he finally pulled back, she wasn't the only one trying to catch her breath. She'd forgotten her rush, and the fact that she hadn't brushed her teeth; she forgot *everything* but him and had turned her wrists so that her hands clasped his hard enough for her nails to leave marks on him.

Straightening, he took a slow, deep breath and let it out, making her realize with some shock and a lot of female pride that he was just as affected as she. "I just wanted to make sure you understand my intentions," he said. "And what I want."

She snorted and rocked against a most impressive erection. "I think I know what you want."

He didn't smile. Not even a twitch of his lips. Instead, his eyes filled with something she couldn't quite catch.

"What I want," he said, "is significantly more than a road trip from hell and a quick relief of some fairly serious sexual tension."

She stared at him. "You mean the relationship you mentioned last night."

"Yes."

"For how long?"

His gaze never left hers. "Until we don't want each other anymore."

She couldn't even imagine not wanting him, and his lips twitched like he could read her mind. Leaning in again, he pressed his mouth to the spot between her breasts.

Over her heart.

"I'm feeling a little self-conscious," she whispered.

"Funny, that's not what I'm feeling."

No kidding. She could feel him hard as stone through his jeans. "I need caffeine," she whispered.

"Here." He handed her the cup.

She sipped, aware of the way his eyes heated every inch of her body as they roamed over her.

Seemed only fair since just the thought of him naked made breathing difficult.

"Better?" he asked.

She managed a nod.

That made him smile. "You're cute in the mornings," he said. "If we had more time, I'd show you just how sexy I find that, but it's time to rise and shine. The roads are open and it's only six o'clock."

"We can get all the way through to Tahoe?"

He smiled. "Merry Christmas, Rory."

Chapter Ten

RORY SPEED SHOWERED and pulled on clothes, and they were out the door not ten minutes later.

"Breakfast?" Max asked, pointing to the small continental spread in the check-in area.

"No," she said. "I'm sorry, I just need to get there."

He didn't say anything until he had them loaded and on the highway. "Need to get there?" he repeated curiously. "Yesterday it was 'want to get there.'"

Yes, and she was extremely aware of the difference. She just didn't want to explain it, how she felt she'd managed to fail her family yet again. She pulled out her phone to call her mom but she still didn't have reception. The curse of the Sierra Mountains.

Max's hand settled on her thigh and then Carl's head came over the seat and settled on her shoulder. Rory's heart warmed from the inside out and she heard herself start talking. "When I told my stepdad I was coming, he had me pick up my mom's present from him. It's a necklace he had special ordered and made in the city. It was supposed to be ready a few days ago but got held up. I told him I'd hand deliver it. He was understandably hesitant to believe me since I haven't been home in so long, but I promised." She paused. "But they always open presents by dawn. I obviously screwed it all up."

"Hold on," Max said. "The present was going to be late anyway, but you offered to pick it up and hand deliver it. You set a deadline on yourself, and now because you missed that you think you failed them? Do I have that right?"

"You don't understand," she said. "I've made promises to come home before and haven't come through. I wanted this to be different."

"It *is* different. You're actually going. And if not for the storm and then my truck and Carl, you'd have been there."

"Not your fault," she said, reaching out to put her hand on his arm. "All those things were out of your control."

He slid her a quick look, his eyes warm. "Yeah, and remember that, Rory. Remember the very same thing. None of this is your fault."

An hour and a half later they made it up and over the summit and into their small Tahoe town. It was just barely eight o'clock. Definitely past her self-imposed deadline, but still early. Hopefully early enough, but her heart was pounding with anxiety.

Max pulled into the driveway of her childhood home. The place was a small ranch-style house, emphasis on *small,* in a neighborhood of hard-working people who didn't spare a lot of time or money on their yards. Not that it mattered because the new snowfall was a white blanket over everything as far as the eye could see, giving new life to the tired street, making it indeed look like Christmas.

"Rory," Max said quietly, once again putting a hand on her thigh. "Breathe."

Right. She'd been holding her breath. She gulped in some air but she was close to a nervous breakdown. Hands sweating, she made herself busy gathering her stuff because a good part of her nerves, she suddenly realized, was from the thought of saying goodbye to Max.

He'd made his interest in her clear but she still felt a moment of panic that she'd somehow misunderstood. "Thanks for the ride," she said quickly as she slid out of the truck, grabbing her bag. "I appreciate—"

Max got out of the truck as well, and then was there, right there at her side, pulling her around to face him. "I'll drive you back to the city whenever you're ready to go."

"I can take the bus—"

"I'll drive you," he said firmly.

"But I don't want to cut your visit with your family short—"

"I'm taking you back," he said right over her. Calm. Sure. Absolutely adamant. "Whatever day and time you want. I'll call you in a little bit to see how you're doing, and you can call me too. Any time." He bent a little to look right into her eyes. "Repeat after me, Rory. Any time."

She stared into his dark green eyes and felt something catch in her heart. Or maybe it was just rolling over and exposing its tender underbelly. "Any time," she whispered.

"Because this isn't over," he said and waited for her to repeat that as well.

"Max—"

"You wanted to give me a Christmas present," he said quietly. "This is it. This is what I want."

"Me?"

"*You.*"

Warmth filled her, and not just her good spots. She felt cherished, wanted, cared for . . . and she felt something else—a huge smile on her face. She couldn't control it. "And I didn't even have to wrap it."

He relaxed and smiled back, and then leaned in for a kiss just as Carl stuck his big head out the truck's still open door and licked Rory from chin to forehead.

She laughed while Max cupped the dog's face in his big palm and pushed him back into the truck. He turned to Rory then, his smile fading as he looked past her to the front door. She followed his gaze and froze at the sight of her stepdad standing on the porch, arms crossed, face creased in the stern frown that had framed her entire youth.

"You're here," he called out. "Thought maybe you'd changed your mind."

Again. He didn't say the word but she felt it shimmering in the air between them. "I didn't." The warm fuzzies of a moment ago were fading fast, leaving her chilled, more than the snow around her. "I'm sorry I'm late, but—"

"No one expected you to get here on any sort of time-table."

Okay, she got it, she was the screw-up once again, but damn. It hurt more than she thought to be on the other side and be judged for who she'd once been. "You don't understand, this time was different—"

"Actually, I do understand and I'm not surprised—"

"Hold on," Max said and grabbed Rory's hand. "You haven't let her talk."

Her stepdad looked at him. "Max Stranton. What are you doing here?"

"I'm Rory's boyfriend," he said so easily that Rory's heart skipped a beat. "The storm slowed us down," Max went on. "The roads were a mess."

"You two okay?" her stepdad asked.

"Yes," Max said. "But we stopped to help an older couple with a flat, and then my dog took off on us. Rory could've gotten a ride from the one car who'd stopped but she stayed to help me find Carl."

Her stepdad looked at Rory.

"I'm sorry if I've disappointed you," she said, "but there was no way I could just take the ride and leave Max alone on the summit in the storm with his dog missing."

"Of course not," her stepdad said.

Rory blinked. Was that . . . understanding in her step-dad's voice? Still stunned at that, she turned to Max when he said her name. He cupped the nape of her neck in a big palm and pulled her in for a quick but warm kiss. "Any time," he said softly. "Yeah?"

"Yeah."

"Even if it's in a few hours."

She let out a half laugh that was more like a sob so she cut it off. "I already told you, I won't cut your visit short—"

"Or yours," her stepdad said. He'd left the front porch and had come closer. "Your mom and sisters are going to be thrilled you made it, Rory."

She looked at him. "Really?"

He gestured with his chin and turned to the front door, where her mom and her three half sisters waited with welcoming smiles on their faces, waving. They were all still in their PJ's, keeping them inside, but at their clear joy at seeing her she felt a lump in her throat.

"It's Christmas," her stepdad said quietly. "And you're actually here. Merry Christmas, Rory. Welcome home. We'll wait inside for you." And then with one look at Max standing strong and tall at her side, he turned and headed back to the house.

Max pulled her into him. "Knew you could handle this."

"How?" she asked in marvel. "I mean, I've been with me for twenty-three years and I still don't get me."

He let out a low laugh and pressed his forehead to hers. "I was a little slow on the uptake, but I've got you now and I don't plan for that to change."

Her breath caught. That sounded a whole lot like her greatest fantasy come true.

"There's one more thing." He nudged her face up. "I love you, Rory. I think I always have."

Emotion flooded her and her knees wobbled. "I need to sit."

Max urged her back a few steps to his still open truck. When she was once again in the passenger seat, he crouched in front of her. "Still with me?"

Her heart had started to pound. She'd never thought to hear the L-word from anyone, much less him, but there it was, out in the open. She should have known it would be like that with him. Honest. Straightforward. She looked into his eyes and nodded. "Still here."

"Did you just nearly pass out when I told you my feelings?" he asked.

"No. I nearly passed out when I realized something."

"What?"

"That I think feel the same way," she whispered like this was a state secret, loving the way it made him smile all the way to his eyes, allowing her to access a well of courage she hadn't known she'd had. She slid her fingers into his hair, which she now knew would make him purr like a cat, a big, wild cat. "I love you, Max." She paused and then let out a small smile as she repeated his vow. "I think I always have."

His low laugh warmed to her to the far corners of her heart and he pulled her in for a tight squeeze. "I'll be back for you. You going to be okay?"

She realized she'd been holding her breath again, for what she had no idea. For him to change his mind?

Laugh? Take it all back? "So . . . that's it?" she asked. "You love me, I love you, the end?"

"For now," he said.

"And later?"

He lifted a shoulder. "We can talk about our next step."

"Which would be . . . ?" she asked.

He kissed the tension away and then pulled back far enough to say, "Whatever you want."

"What about what you want?" she asked, breathless. She was pretty sure he kissed her just to leave her in a state.

He stroked the hair from her face. "I want it all."

Oh. Well, that sounded . . . promising. And exciting. She was so happy she yanked him in and kissed him until both of them were breathless. "Merry Christmas," she whispered against his lips. "I'll give you your *real* present later."

He smiled sexily. "Sounds promising."

She smiled back. "It is."

Read on for a look at the other fun
and sexy Heartbreaker Bay novels

SWEET LITTLE LIES

THE TROUBLE WITH MISTLETOE

Available now from Avon Books!

And an exclusive sneak peek of

ACCIDENTALLY ON PURPOSE

Coming January 2017!

#KeepCalmAndRideAUnicorn

PRU HARRIS'S MOM had taught her to make wishes on pink cars, falling leaves, and brass lamps, because wishing on something as ordinary as stars or wishing wells was a sign of no imagination.

Clearly the woman standing not three feet away in the light mist, searching her purse for change to toss into the courtyard fountain hadn't been raised by a hippie mom as Pru had been.

Not that it mattered, since her mom had been wrong. Wishes, along with things like winning the lotto or finding a unicorn, never happened in real life.

The woman, shielding her eyes from the light rain

with one hand, holding a coin in her other, sent Pru a wry grimace. "I know it's silly, but it's a hit-rock-bottom thing."

Something Pru understood all too well. She set a wriggly Thor down and shook her arms to try and bring back some circulation. Twenty-five pounds of wet, tubby, afraid-of-his-own-shadow mutt had felt like seventy-five by the end of their thirty-minute walk home from work.

Thor objected to being on the wet ground with a sharp bark. Thor didn't like rain.

Or walking.

But he loved Pru more than life itself so he stuck close, his tail wagging slowly as he watched her face to determine what mood they were in.

The woman blinked and stared down at Thor. "Oh," she said, surprised. "I thought it was a really fat cat."

Thor's tail stopped wagging and he barked again, as if to prove that not only was he all dog, he was big, *badass* dog.

Because Thor—a rescue of undetermined breed—also believed he was a bullmastiff.

When the woman took a step back, Pru sighed and picked him back up again. His old man face was creased into a protective frown, his front paws dangling, his tail back to wagging now that he was suddenly tall. "Sorry," Pru said. "He can't see well and it makes him grumpy, but he's not a cat." She gave Thor a *behave* squeeze. "He only acts like one."

Thor volleyed back a look that said Pru might want to not leave her favorite shoes unattended tonight.

The woman's focus turned back to the fountain and she eyed the quarter in her hand. "They say it's never too late to wish on love, right?"

"Right," Pru said. Because they did say that. And just because in her own personal experience love had proven even rarer than unicorns didn't mean she'd step on someone else's hopes and dreams.

A sudden bolt of lightning lit up the San Francisco skyline like the Fourth of July. Except it was June, and cold as the Arctic. Thor squeaked and shoved his face into Pru's neck. Pru started to count but didn't even get to One-Mississippi before the thunder boomed loud enough to make them all jump.

"Yikes." The woman dropped the quarter back into her purse. "Not even love's worth getting electrocuted." And she ran off.

Pru and Thor did the same, heading across the cobblestone courtyard. Normally she took her time here, enjoying the glorious old architecture of the building, the corbeled brick and exposed iron trusses, the big windows, but the rain had begun to fall in earnest now, hitting so hard that the drops bounced back up to her knees. In less than ten seconds, she was drenched through, her clothes clinging to her skin, filling her ankle boots so that they squished with each step.

"Slow down, sweetness!" someone called out. It was the old homeless guy who was usually in the alley. With his skin tanned to the consistency of leather and his long, wispy white cotton-ball hair down to the collar of his loud pineapples-and-parrots Hawaiian shirt, he looked like Doc from *Back to the Future*, plus a few decades. A century tops. "You can't get much wetter," he said.

But Pru wasn't actually trying to dodge the weather, she loved the rain. She was trying to dodge her demons, something she was beginning to suspect couldn't be done.

"Gotta get to my apartment," she said, breathless from her mad dash. When she'd hit twenty-six, her spin class instructor had teasingly told her that it was all downhill from here on out, she hadn't believed him. Joke was on her.

"What's the big rush?"

Resigned to a chat, Pru stopped. Old Guy was sweet and kind, even if he had refused to tell her his name, claiming to have forgotten it way back in the seventies. True or not, she'd been feeding him since she'd moved into this building three weeks ago. "The cable company's finally coming today," she said. "They said five o'clock."

"That's what they told you yesterday. And last week," he said, trying to pet Thor, who wasn't having any of it.

Another thing on Thor's hate list—men.

"But this time they mean it," Pru said and set Thor down. At least that's what the cable company supervisor had promised Pru on the phone, and she needed cable TV. Bad. The finals of *So You Think You Can Dance* were on tomorrow night.

"'Scuse me," someone said as he came from the elevator well and started to brush past her. He wore a hat low over his eyes to keep the rain out of his face and the cable company's logo on his pec. He was carrying a toolbox and looking peeved by life in general.

Thor began a low growl deep in his throat while hiding

behind Pru's legs. He sounded fierce, but he looked ridiculous, especially wet. He had the fur of a Yorkshire terrier—if that Yorkshire terrier was fat—even though he was really a complete Heinz 57. And hell, maybe he *was* part cat. Except that only one of his ears folded over. The other stood straight up, giving him a perpetually confused look.

No self-respecting cat would have allowed such a thing. In fact, the cable guy took one look at him and snorted, and then kept moving.

"Wait!" Pru yelled after him. "Are you looking for 3C?"

He stopped, his gaze running over her, slowing at her torso. "Actually," he said. "I'm more a double D man myself."

Pru looked down at herself. Her shirt had suctioned itself to her breasts. Narrowing her eyes, she crossed her arms over her decidedly not DDs. "Let me be more clear," she said, tightening her grip on Thor's leash because he was still growling, although he was doing it very quietly because he only wanted to pretend to be a tough guy. "Are you looking for the person who lives in *apartment* 3C?"

"I was but no one's home." He eyed Thor. "Is that a dog?"

"Yes! And *I'm* 3C," Pru said. "I'm home!"

He shook his head. "You didn't answer your door."

"I will now, I promise." She pulled her keys from her bag. "We can just run up there right now and—"

"No can do, dude. It's five o'clock straight up." He waved his watch to prove it. "I'm off the clock."

"But—"

But nothing, he was gone, walking off into the downpour, vanishing into the fog like they were on the set of a horror flick.

Thor stopped growling.

"Great," Pru muttered. "Just great."

Old Guy slid his dentures around some. "I could hook up your cable for you. I've seen someone do it once or twice."

The old man, like the old Pacific Heights building around them, had seen better days, but both held a certain old-fashioned charm—which didn't mean she trusted him inside her apartment. "Thanks," she said. "But this is for the best. I don't really need cable TV all that bad."

"But the finals of *So You Think You Can Dance* are on tomorrow night."

She sighed. "I know."

Another bolt of lightning lit the sky, and again was immediately followed by a crack of thunder that echoed off the courtyard's stone walls and shook the ground beneath their feet.

"That's my exit," Old Guy said and disappeared into the alley.

Pru got Thor upstairs, rubbed him down with a towel and tucked him into his bed. She'd thought she wanted the same for herself, but she was hungry and there was nothing good in her refrigerator. So she quickly changed into dry clothes and went back downstairs.

Still raining.

One of these days she was going to buy an umbrella. For now, she made the mad dash toward the northeast corner of the building, past the Coffee Bar, the Waffle Shop, and the South Bark Mutt Shop—all closed, past The Canvas tattoo studio—open—and went straight for the Irish Pub.

Without the lure of cable to make her evening, she needed chicken wings.

And nobody made chicken wings like O'Riley's.

It's not the chicken wings you're wanting, a small voice inside her head said. And that was fact. Nope, what drew her into O'Riley's like a bee to honey was the six-foot, broad-shouldered, dark eyes, dark smile of Finn O'Riley himself.

From her three weeks in the building, she knew the people who lived and/or worked here were tight. And she knew that it was in a big part thanks to Finn because he was the glue, the steady one.

She knew more too. More than she should.

"Hey!" Old Guy stuck his head out of the alley. "If you're getting us wings, don't forget extra sauce!"

She waved at him, and once again dripping wet, entered O'Riley's where she stood for a second getting her bearings.

Okay, that was a total lie. She stood there *pretending* to get her bearings while her gaze sought out the bar and the guys behind it.

There were two of them working tonight. Twenty-two-year-old Sean was flipping bottles, juggling them to the catcalls and wild amusement of a group of women all belly up to the bar, wooing them with his wide smile and laughing eyes. But he wasn't the one Pru's gaze gravitated to like he was a rack of double-stuffed Oreo cookies.

Nope, that honor went to the guy who ran the place, Sean's older brother. All lean muscle and easy confidence, Finn O'Riley wasn't pandering to the crowd. He never did. He moved quickly and efficiently without show, quietly hustling to fill the orders, keeping an eye on the kitchen, as always steady as a rock under pressure, doing all the real work.

Pru could watch him all day. It was his hands, she'd decided, they were constantly moving with expert precision. He was busy, way too busy for her, of course, which was only one of the many reasons why she hadn't allowed herself to fantasize about him doing deliciously naughty, wicked things to her in her bed.

Whoops. That was another big fat lie.

She'd *totally* fantasized about him doing deliciously naughty, wicked things to her in bed. And also out of it.

He was her unicorn.

He bent low behind the bar for something and an entire row of women seated on the barstools leaned in unison for a better view. Meerkats on parade.

When he straightened a few seconds later, he was hoisting a huge crate of something, maybe clean glasses, and not looking like he was straining too much either. This was in no doubt thanks to all that lean, hard muscle visible beneath his black tee and faded jeans. His biceps bulged as he turned, allowing her to see that his Levi's fit him perfectly, front *and* back.

If he noticed his avid audience, he gave no hint of it. He merely set the crate down on the counter, and ignoring the women ogling him, nodded a silent hello in Pru's direction.

She stilled and then craned her neck, looking behind her.

No one there. Just herself, dripping all over his floor.

She turned back and found Finn looking quietly amused. Their gazes locked and held for a long beat, like maybe he was taking her pulse from across the room, absorbing the fact that she was drenched and breathless. The corners of his mouth twitched. She'd amused him again.

People shifted between them. The place was crowded as always, but when the way was clear again, Finn was still looking at her, steady and unblinking, those dark green eyes flickering with something other than amusement now, something that began to warm her from the inside out.

Three weeks and it was the same every single time . . .

Pru considered herself fairly brave and maybe a little more than fairly adventurous—but not necessarily forward. It wasn't easy for her to connect with people.

Which was the only excuse she had for jerking her gaze away, pretending to eye the room.

The pub itself was small and cozy. One half bar, the other half pub designated for dining, the décor was dark woods reminiscent of an old thatched inn. The tables were made from whiskey barrels and the bar itself had been crafted out of repurposed longhouse-style doors. The hanging brass lantern lights and stained-glass fixtures along with the horse-chewed, old-fence base-boards finished the look that said antique charm and friendly warmth.

Music drifted out of invisible speakers, casting a jovial mood, but not too loud so as to make conversation difficult. There was a wall of windows and also a rack of accordion wood and glass doors that opened the pub on both sides, one to the courtyard, the other to the street, giving a view down the hill to the beautiful Fort Mason Park and Marina Green, and the Golden Gate Bridge behind that.

All of which was fascinating, but not nearly as fascinating as Finn himself, which meant that her eyes, the traitors, swiveled right back to him.

He pointed at her.

"Me?" she asked, even though he couldn't possibly hear her from across the place.

With a barely there smile, he gave her a finger crook.

Yep. Her.

The Trouble With Mistletoe
Chapter 1

#TheTroubleWithMistletoe

THE SUN HAD barely come up and Willa Davis was already elbow deep in puppies and poo—a typical day for her. As owner of the South Bark Mutt Shop, she spent much of her time scrubbing, cajoling, primping, hoisting—and more cajoling. She wasn't above bribing either.

Which meant she kept pet treats in her pockets, making her irresistible to any and all four-legged creatures within scent range. A shame though that a treat hadn't yet been invented to make her irresistible to *two*-legged male creatures as well. Now *that* would've been handy.

But then again, she'd put herself on a Man-Time-Out so she didn't need such a thing.

"Wuff!"

This from one of the pups she was bathing. The little guy wobbled in close and licked her chin.

"That's not going to butter me up," she said, but it totally did and unable to resist that face she returned the kiss on the top of his cute little nose.

One of Willa's regular grooming clients had brought in her eight-week-old heathens—er, golden retriever puppies.

Six of them.

It was over an hour before the shop would open at nine a.m. but her client had called in a panic because the pups had rolled in horse poo. God knew where they'd found horse poo in the Cow Hollow district of San Francisco—maybe a policeman's horse had left an undignified pile in the street—but they were a mess.

And now so was Willa.

Two puppies, even three, were manageable, but handling six by herself bordered on insanity. "Okay, listen up," she said to the squirming, happily panting puppies in the large tub in her grooming room. "Everyone sit."

One and Two sat. Three climbed up on top of the both of them and shook his tubby little body, drenching Willa in the process.

Meanwhile, Four, Five, and Six made a break for it, paws pumping, ears flopping over their eyes, tails wagging wildly as they scrabbled, climbing over each other like circus tumblers to get out of the tub.

"Rory?" Willa called out. "Could use another set of hands back here." Or three . . .

No answer. Either her twenty-three-year-old employee had her headphones cranked up to make-me-deaf-please or she was on Instagram and didn't want to lose her place. *"Rory!"*

The girl finally poked her head around the corner, phone in hand, screen lit.

Yep. Instagram.

"Holy crap," Rory said, eyes wide. "Literally."

Willa looked down at herself. Yep, her apron and clothes were splattered with suds and water and a few other questionable stains that might or might not be related to the horse poo. She'd lay money down on the fact that her layered strawberry blonde hair had rioted, resembling an explosion in a down-pillow factory. Good thing she'd forgone makeup at the early emergency call so at least she didn't have mascara running down her face. "Help."

Rory cheerfully dug right in, not shying from getting wet or dirty. Dividing and conquering, they got all the pups out of the tub, dried, and back in their baby pen in twenty minutes. One through Five fell into the instant slumber that only babies and the very drunk could achieve, but Six remained stubbornly awake, climbing over his siblings determined to get back into Willa's arms.

Laughing, she scooped the little guy up. His legs bicycled in the air, tail wagging faster than the speed of light, taking his entire hind end with it.

"Not sleepy, huh?" Willa asked.

He strained toward her, clearly wanting to lick her face.

"Oh no you don't. I know where that tongue's been." Tucking him under her arm, she carted him out front to the retail portion of her shop, setting him into another baby pen with some puppy toys, one that was visible to street traffic. "Now sit there and look pretty and bring in some customers, would you?"

Panting with happiness, the puppy pounced on a toy and got busy playing as Willa went through her opening routine, flipping on the lights throughout the retail area. The shop came to life, mostly thanks to the insane amount of holiday decorations she'd put up the week before, including the seven-foot tree in the front corner— lit to within an inch of its life.

"It's only the first of December and it looks like Christmas threw up in here," Rory said from the doorway.

Willa looked around at her dream-come-true shop, the one finally operating in the black. Well, most of the time. "But in a classy way, right?"

Rory eyed the one hundred miles of strung lights and more boughs of holly than even the North Pole should have. "Um . . . right."

Willa ignored the doubtful sarcasm. One, Rory hadn't grown up in a stable home. And two, neither had she. For the both of them Christmas had always been a luxury that, like three squares and a roof, had been out of their reach more than not. They'd each dealt with that differently. Rory didn't need the pomp and circumstance of the holidays.

Willa did, desperately. So yeah, she was twenty-seven years old and still went overboard for the holidays.

"Ohmigod," Rory said, staring at their newest cash register display. "Is that a rack of penis headbands?"

"No!" Willa laughed. "It's reindeer-antler headbands for dogs."

Rory stared at her.

Willa grimaced. "Okay, so maybe I went a little crazy—"

"A *little*?"

"Ha-ha," Willa said, picking up a reindeer-antler headband. It didn't look like a penis to her, but then again it'd been a while since she'd seen one up close and personal. "These are going to sell like hotcakes, mark my words."

"Ohmigod—don't put it on!" Rory said in sheer horror as Willa did just that.

"It's called marketing." Willa rolled her eyes upward to take in the antlers jutting up above her head. "Shit."

Rory grinned and pointed to the swear jar that Willa had set up to keep them all in line. Mostly her, actually. They used the gained cash for their muffins and coffee fix.

Willa slapped a dollar into it. "I guess the antlers do look a little like penises," she admitted. "Or is it peni? What's the plural of penis?"

"Pene?" Rory asked and they both cracked up.

Willa got a hold of herself. "Clearly I'm in need of Tina's caffeine, *bad*."

"I'll go," Rory said. "I caught sight of her coming through the courtyard at the crack of dawn wearing six-inch wedge sneakers, her hair teased to the North Pole, making her look, like, eight feet tall."

Tina used to be Tim and everyone in the five-story, offbeat historical Pacific Pier Building had enjoyed Tim—but they *loved* Tina. Tina rocked.

"What's your order?" Rory asked.

Tina's coffees came in themes and Willa knew just what she needed for the day ahead. "One of her It's Way Too Early for Life's Nonsense." She pulled some more cash from her pocket and this time a handful of puppy treats came out too, bouncing all over the floor.

"And to think, you can't get a date," Rory said dryly.

"Not *can't* get a date," Willa corrected. "Don't want a date. I pick the wrong men, something I'm not alone in . . ."

Rory blew out a sigh at the truth of that statement and then went brows up when Willa's stomach growled like a roll of thunder.

"Okay, so grab me a muffin as well." Tina made the best muffins on the planet. "Make it two. Or better yet, three. No, wait." Her jeans had been hard to button that morning. "Crap, three muffins would be my entire day's calories. One," she said firmly. "One muffin for me and make it a blueberry so it counts as a serving of fruit."

"Got it," Rory said. "A coffee, a blueberry muffin, and a straitjacket on the side."

"Ha-ha. Now get out of here before I change my order again."

South Bark had two doors, one that opened to the street, the other to the building's courtyard with its beautiful cobblestones and the historical old fountain that Willa could never resist tossing a coin into and wishing for true love as she passed.

Rory headed out the courtyard door.

"Hey," Willa said. "If there's any change, throw a coin into the fountain for me?"

"So you're on a self-imposed man embargo but you still want to wish on true love?"

"Yes, please."

Rory shook her head. "It's your dime." She didn't believe in wishes or wasting even a quarter, but she obediently headed out.

When she was gone, Willa's smile faded. Each of her three part-time employees was young and they all had one thing in common.

Life had churned them up and spit them out at a young age, leaving them out there in the big, bad world all alone.

Since Willa had been one of those lost girls herself, she collected them. She gave them jobs and advice that they only listened to about half the time.

But she figured fifty percent was better than zero percent.

Her most recent hire was nineteen-year-old Lyndie, who was still a little feral but they were working on that. Then there was Cara, who'd come a long way. Rory had been with Willa the longest. The girl put up a strong front but she still struggled. Proof positive was the fading markings of a bruise on her jaw where her ex-boyfriend had knocked her into a doorjamb.

Just the thought had Willa clenching her fists. Sometimes at night she dreamed about what she'd like to do to the guy. High on the list was cutting off his twig and berries with a dull knife but she had an aversion to jail.

Rory deserved better. Tough as nails on the outside, she was a tender marshmallow on the inside, and she'd do anything for Willa. It was sweet, but also a huge responsibility because Rory looked to Willa for her normal.

A daunting prospect on the best of days.

She checked on Six and found the puppy finally fast asleep sprawled on his back, feet spread wide to show the world his most prized possessions.

Just like a man for you.

Next she checked on his siblings. Also asleep. Feeling like the mother of sextuplets, she tiptoed back out to the front and opened her laptop, planning to inventory the new boxes of supplies she'd received late the night before.

She'd just gotten knee-deep in four different twenty-five-pound sacks of bird feed—she still couldn't believe how many people in San Francisco had birds—when someone knocked on the front glass door.

Damn. It was only a quarter after eight but it went against the grain to turn away a paying customer. Straightening, she swiped her hands on her apron and looked up.

A guy stood on the other side of the glass, mouth grim, expression dialed to Tall, Dark, and Attitude-ridden. He was something too, all gorgeous and broody and—hold up. There was something familiar about him, enough that her feet propelled her forward out of pure curiosity. When it hit her halfway to the door, she froze, her heart just about skidding to a stop.

"Keane Winters," she murmured, lip curling like she'd just eaten a black licorice. She hated black licorice. But she was looking at the only man on the planet who could make her feel all puckered up as well as good about her decision to give up men.

In fact, if she'd only given them up sooner, say back on the day of the Sadie Hawkins dance in her freshman year of high school when he'd stood her up, she'd have saved herself a lot of heartache in the years since.

On the other side of the door, Keane shoved his mirrored sunglasses to the top of his head, revealing dark chocolate eyes that she knew could melt when he was amused or feeling flirtatious, or turn to ice when he was so inclined.

They were ice now.

Catching her gaze, he lifted a cat carrier. A bright pink bedazzled carrier.

He had a cat.

Her entire being wanted to soften at this knowledge because that meant on some level at least he had to be a good guy, right?

Luckily her brain clicked on, remembering everything, every little detail of that long ago night. Like how she'd had to borrow a dress for the dance from a girl in her class who'd gleefully lorded it over her, how she'd had to beg her foster mother to let her go, how she'd stolen a Top Ramen from the locked pantry and eaten it dry in the bathroom so she wouldn't have to buy both her dinner and his, as was custom for the "backward" dance.

"We're closed," she said through the still locked glass door.

Not a word escaped his lips. He simply raised the cat carrier another inch, like he was God's gift.

And he had been. At least in high school.

Wishing she'd gotten some caffeine before dealing with this, she blew out a breath and stepped closer, annoyed at her eyes because they refused to leave his as she unlocked and then opened the door. Just another customer, she told herself. One that had ruined her life like it was nothing without so much as an apology . . . "Morning," she said, determined to be polite.

Not a single flicker of recognition crossed his face and she found something even more annoying than this man being on her doorstep.

The fact that she'd been so forgettable he didn't even remember her.

"I'm closed until nine." She said this in her most pleasant voice although a little bit of eff-you *might've* been implied.

"I've got to be at work by nine," he said. "I want to board a cat for the day."

Keane had always been big and intimidating. It was what had made him such an effective jock. He'd ruled on the football field, the basketball court, *and* the baseball diamond. The perfect trifecta, the all-around package.

Every girl in the entire school—and also a good amount of the teachers—had spent an indecent amount of time eyeballing that package.

But just as Willa had given up men, she'd even longer

ago given up thinking about that time, inarguably the worst years of her life. While Keane had been off breaking records and winning hearts, she'd been drowning under the pressures of school and work, not to mention basic survival.

She got that it wasn't his fault her memories of that time were horrific. Nor was it his fault that just looking at him brought them all back to her. But emotions weren't logical. "I'm sorry," she said, "but I'm all full up today."

"I'll pay double."

He had a voice like fine whiskey. Not that she ever drank fine whiskey. Even the cheap stuff was a treat. And maybe it was just her imagination, but she was having a hard time getting past the fact that he was both the same and yet had changed. He was still tall, of course, and built sexy as hell, damn him. Broad shoulders, lean hips, biceps straining his shirt as he held up the cat carrier.

He wore faded ripped jeans on his long legs and scuffed work boots. His only concession to the San Francisco winter was a long-sleeved T-shirt that enhanced all those ripped muscles and invited her to BITE ME in big block letters across his chest.

She wasn't going to lie to herself, she kind of wanted to. *Hard.*

He stood there exuding raw, sexual power and energy—not that she was noticing. Nor was she taking in his expression that said maybe he'd already had a bad day.

He could join her damn club.

And at that thought, she mentally smacked herself in

the forehead. No! There would be *no* club joining. She'd set boundaries for herself. She was Switzerland. Neutral. No importing or exporting of anything including sexy smoldering glances, hot body parts, *nothing*.

Period.

Especially not with Keane Winters, thank you very much. And anyway, she didn't board animals for the general public. Yes, sometimes she boarded as special favors for clients, a service she called "fur-babysitting" because her capacity here was too small for official boarding. If and when she agreed to "babysit" overnight as a favor, it meant taking her boarders home with her, so she was extremely selective.

And handsome men who'd once been terribly mean boys who ditched painfully shy girls after she'd summoned up every ounce of her courage to ask him out to a dance did *not* fit her criteria. "I don't board—" she started, only to be interrupted by an unholy howl from inside the pink cat carrier.

It was automatic for her to reach for it, and Keane readily released it with what looked to be comical relief.

Turning her back on him, Willa carried the carrier to the counter, incredibly aware that Keane followed her through her shop, moving with an unusually easy grace for such a big guy.

The cat was continuously howling now so she quickly unzipped the carrier, expecting the animal inside to be dying giving the level of unhappiness it'd displayed.

The earsplitting caterwauling immediately stopped and a huge Siamese cat blinked vivid blue eyes owlishly up at her. It had a pale, creamy coat with a darker facial mask that matched its black ears, legs, and paws.

"Well aren't you beautiful," Willa said softly and slipped her hands into the box.

The cat immediately allowed herself to be lifted, pressing her face into Willa's throat for a cuddle.

"Aw," Willa said gently. "It's alright now, I've got you. You just hated that carrier, didn't you?"

"What the ever-loving hell," Keane said, hands on hips now as he glared at the cat. "Are you kidding me?"

"What?"

He scowled. "My great-aunt's sick and needs help. She dropped the cat off with me last night."

Well, damn. That was a pretty nice thing he'd done, taking the cat in for his sick aunt.

"The minute Sally left," Keane went on, "this thing went gonzo."

Willa looked down at the cat, who gazed back at her, quiet, serene, positively angelic. "What did she do?"

Keane snorted. "What *didn't* she do would be the better question. She hid under my bed and tore up my mattress. Then she helped herself to everything on my counters, knocking stuff to the floor, destroying my laptop and tablet and phone all in one fell swoop. And then she . . ." He trailed off and appeared to chomp on his back teeth.

"What?"

"Took a dump in my favorite running shoes."

Willa did her best not to laugh out loud and say "good girl." It took her a minute. "Maybe she's just upset to be away from home, and missing your aunt. Cats are creatures of habit. They don't like change." She spoke to Keane without taking her gaze off the cat, not wanting to look into the dark, mesmerizing eyes that didn't recognize her because if she did, she might be tempted to pick one of the tiaras displayed on her counter and hit him over the head with it.

"What's her name?" she asked.

"Petunia, but I'm going with Pita. Short for pain in the ass."

Willa stroked along the cat's back and Petunia pressed into her hand for more. A low and rumbly purr filled the room and Petunia's eyes slitted with pleasure.

Keane let out a breath as Willa continued to pet her. "Unbelievable," he said. "You're wearing catnip as perfume, right?"

Willa raised an eyebrow. "Is that the only reason you think she'd like me?"

"Yes."

Okay then. Willa opened her mouth to end this little game and tell him that she wasn't doing this, but then she looked into Petunia's deep-as-the-ocean blue eyes and felt her heart stir. *Crap.* "Fine," she heard herself say. "If you can provide proof of rabies and FVRCP vaccinations, I'll take her for today only."

"Thank you," he said with such genuine feeling, she glanced up at him.

A mistake.

His dark eyes had warmed to the color of melted dark chocolate. "One question."

"What?" she asked warily.

"Do you always wear X-rated headbands?"

Her hands flew to her head. She'd completely forgotten she was wearing the penis headband. "Are you referring to my reindeer antlers?"

"Reindeer antlers," he repeated.

"That's right."

"Whatever you say." He was smiling now, and of course the rat-fink bastard had a sexy-as-hell smile. And unbelievably her good parts stood up and took notice. Clearly her body hadn't gotten the memo on the no-man thing. Especially not *this* man.

"My name's Keane by the way," he said. "Keane Winters."

He paused, clearly expecting her to tell him her name in return, but she had a dilemma now. If she told him who she was and he suddenly recognized her, he'd also remember exactly how pathetic she'd once been. And if he *didn't* recognize her then that meant she was even more forgettable than she'd thought and she'd have to throw the penis headband at him after all.

"And you are . . . ?" he asked, rich voice filled with amusement at her pause.

Well, hell. Now or never, she supposed. "Willa Davis," she said and held her breath.

There was no change in his expression whatsoever. Forgettable then, and she ground her back teeth for a minute.

"I appreciate you doing this for me, Willa," he said.

She had to consciously unclench her teeth to speak.

"I'm not doing it for you. I'm doing it for Petunia," she said, wanting to be crystal clear. "And you'll need to be back here to pick her up before closing."

"Deal."

"I've got a few questions for you," she said. "Like an emergency contact, your driver's license info, and"—God help her, she was going to hell if she asked this but she couldn't help herself, she wanted to jog his memory—"where you went to high school."

He arched a brow. "High school?"

"Yes, you never know what's going to be important."

He looked amused. "As long as I don't have to wear a headband of dicks, you can have whatever info you need."

Five extremely long minutes later he'd filled out the required form and provided the information needed after a quick call to his aunt—all apparently without getting his memory jogged. Then, with one last amused look at her reindeer antlers a.k.a. penis headband, he walked out the door.

Willa was still watching him go when Rory came to stand next to her, casually sipping her coffee as she handed over Willa's.

"Are we looking at his ass?" Rory wanted to know.

Yes, and to Willa's eternal annoyance, it was the best ass she'd ever seen. How unfair was that? The least he could've done was get some pudge. "Absolutely not."

"Well we're missing out, because *wow*."

Willa looked at her. "He's too old for you."

"He's thirty. What," she said at Willa's raised brow. "You've got the copy of his driver's license right here on the counter. I did the math, that's not a crime. And anyway, you're right, he's old. Really *old*."

"You do realize I'm only a few years behind him."

"You're old too," Rory said and nudged her shoulder to Willa's.

The equivalent of a big, fat, mushy hug.

"And for the record," the girl went on, "I was noticing his ass for *you*."

"Ha," Willa said. "The devil himself couldn't drag my old, dead corpse out on a date with him, even if he is hot as balls. I gave up men, remember? That's who I am right now, a woman who doesn't need a man."

"Who you are is a stubborn, obstinate woman who has a lot of love to give but is currently imitating a chicken. But hey, if you wanna let your past bad judgment calls rule your world and live like a nun, carry on just as you are."

"Gee," Willa said dryly. "Thanks."

"You're welcome. But I reserve the right to question your IQ. I hear you lose IQ points when you get old." She smiled sweetly. "Maybe you should start taking that Centrum Silver or something. Want me to run out and get some?"

Willa threw the penis headband at her, but Rory, being a youngster and all, successfully ducked in time.

Accidentally on Purpose
Chapter 1

#TakeMeToYourLeader

IT WAS A good thing Elle Wheaton loved being in charge and ordering people around, because if it wasn't for the thrill of having both those things in her job description, she absolutely didn't get paid enough to handle all the idiots in her world. "Last night was a disaster," she said.

Her boss, not looking nearly as concerned as she, shrugged. He was many things and one of them was the owner of the Pacific Pier Building in which they stood, located in the Cow Hollow district of San Francisco. A detail he preferred to keep to himself.

In fact, only one person besides herself knew his identity, but as the building's general manager, Elle alone handled everything and was always his go-between. The calm, *kickass* go-between, if she said so herself, although what had happened last night had momentarily shaken some of her calm.

"I have faith in you," he said.

She slid him a look. "In other words, 'Fix it, Elle, because I don't want to be bothered about it.'"

"Well, and that," he said with a smile as he pushed his glasses further up on his nose.

She refused to be charmed. Yes, he was sexy in that utterly oblivious way of smart geeks and, yes, they were best friends and she loved him, but in her world, love had limits. "Maybe I should recap the disaster for you," she said. "First, the little lights in every emergency exit sign in the entire building died at midnight. So when Mrs. Winslowe in 3D went to take her geriatric dog to do his business, she couldn't see the stairwell. Cut to Mr. Nottingham from 4A—whom, it should be noted, was sneaking out of his mistress's apartment in 3F— slipping and falling in dog poo."

"You can't make this stuff up," he said, still smiling.

Elle crossed her arms. "Mr. Nottingham broke his ankle and very nearly his ass, requiring an ambulance ride and a possible lawsuit. And you're amused."

"Come on, Elle. You and I both know life sucks golf balls if you let it. Gotta find the fun somewhere. We'll pay the hospital bill and buy Mr. Nottingham new pants. I'll throw in a weekend getaway and he can take his girlfriend or his wife—or both if he wants. We'll make it right." Spence smiled at her snort. "Get yourself some caffeine. You look like you're down a pint."

"My life isn't normal," she said with a shake of her head.

"Forget normal. Normal's overrated. Now drink that gross green stuff you can't survive without."

"It's just tea, you weirdo. And I could totally survive without it if I needed to." She paused. "I just can't guarantee anyone else's safety."

"Exactly, so why take chances?"

Elle rolled her eyes. She was still taking what had happened last night personally. She knew everyone in this building, each and every business on the first and second floor and every tenant on the third and fourth floor, and she felt responsible for all of them.

And someone had been hurt on her watch. Unacceptable. "You do realize that the emergency exit system falls under security's jurisdiction," she said. "Which means the security company you hired failed us."

Spence, following her line of thought, stopped looking so amused. He put down his coffee. "No, Elle."

"Spence, a year ago now you sought me out for the general manager job. You put me in charge of covering your ass, which we both know I'm very good at. So I'm going to go discuss this matter with Archer, your head of security."

He grimaced. "At least let me clear the building before you two go at each other."

"There won't be a fight." At least not that she'd tell him about. "I'm simply doing my job and that includes managing one Archer Hunt."

"Yes, technically," Spence allowed. "But we both know that he answers to no one but himself and he certainly doesn't consider you his boss. He doesn't consider *anyone* his boss."

Elle smiled and mainlined some more tea, the nectar of the gods as far as she was concerned. "His problem, not mine."

Looking pained, Spence stood. "He's not going to enjoy you going off on him this early half-cocked, Elle."

"Ask me if I care."

"*I* care," Spence said. "It's too early to help you bury his body."

Elle let out a short laugh. Her and Archer's antagonistic attitude toward each other had been well documented. The thing was, Archer thought he ran the world, including her.

But no one ran her world except her. "If everyone would just do what they were supposed to and stay out of my way . . ." she said, trailing off because Spence was no longer listening to her. Instead he was staring out the window, his leanly muscled body suddenly tense, prompting her to his side to see what had caught his interest.

A woman was coming out of the coffee shop and Spence was staring at her. It was his ex, who had once upon a time done her best to rip out his heart.

"Want me to have her kicked off the premises?" Elle asked. "Or I could have her investigated and found guilty of a crime." She was just kidding. Mostly.

"I don't need you to handle my damn dates."

Given that he was a walking Fortune 500 company and also that he'd been badly burned, he actually did need his women investigated, but Elle didn't argue with him. Arguing with Spence was like arguing with a brick wall. But he hadn't dated since his ex and it had been months and months, and her heart squeezed because he was gun-shy now. "Hey, in case you haven't heard, hot genius mechanical engineers slash geeks are in. You'll find someone better." Much better, if she had her say . . .

He still didn't respond and Elle rolled her eyes. "How come men are idiots?"

"Because women don't come with instruction manuals." He pushed away from the window. "I've gotta go. No killing anyone today, Elle."

"Sure."

He took the time to give her a long look.

She sighed. "Fine. I won't kill Archer."

When she was alone, she finished her tea, applied some lip gloss—for herself, mind you, not for Archer—and left her office, taking her time walking the open hallway. She loved this building and never got tired of admiring the unique architecture of the old place; the corbeled brick and exposed iron trusses, the long picture windows in each unit, the cobblestone courtyard below with the huge fountain where idiots came from all over San Francisco and beyond to toss their money and wish for love.

She was on the second floor in the far north corner, from which if she pressed her nose up against her office window and if there wasn't any fog, she could see down the hill to the Marina Green and the bay with a very tiny slice of the Golden Gate Bridge as well.

She tried to play it cool, but even after a whole year it was a thrill to live in the heart of the city. Although she hadn't grown up far from here, it'd been a world away and at least ten rungs down on the social ladder.

It was still early enough that the place was quiet. As she passed the elevator, the doors opened and the woman in charge of housekeeping services came through pushing a large cart.

"Hey, honey," Trudy said in her been-smoking-for-three-decades voice. "Need anything?"

"Nope, I'm good." Good plus mad, but although she adored Trudy, the woman couldn't keep a secret to save her life. "Just taking in the nice morning."

"Oh, that's a disappointment," Trudy said. "I thought maybe you were looking for that hottie with the nice package, the one who runs the investigation firm down the hall."

Elle nearly choked on her tea. "Nice *package?*"

"Well I'm old, not dead." And with a wink, Trudy pushed her cart down the hall.

It was true that Archer was annoyingly hot, not that she cared. Hot was useless to her. She'd much rather have the things that had eluded her for most of her life—safety, security . . . stability.

Three things Archer had never been accused of.

At the other end of the hall, she stopped in front of the door with a discreet sign: HUNT INVESTIGATIONS.

The investigative and elite security firm was carried

on Archer's reputation alone, no ads or marketing required. Basically Archer and the men he employed were finders and fixers, independent contractors for hire, and not necessarily tied by the same red tape as the law.

Which worked for Archer. Rules had never been his thing.

She opened the door and let herself into the reception area, which was much bigger than hers. Clean, masculine lines. Large furniture. Wide open space. A glass partition separated the front from the inner offices.

The check-in counter was empty. The receptionist wasn't in yet—it was too early for Mollie. But not for the other employees. Past the glass Elle could see part of the inner office. A group of men, five of them, entered by a private door. They'd clearly just come back from some sort of job that had required them to be locked and loaded since they currently looked like a SWAT team.

Elle literally stopped short. And if she was being honest, her heart stopped too because sweet baby Jesus. The lot of them stood there stripping off weapons and shirts so that all she could see was a mass of mind-blowing bodies, sweaty and tatted and in all varieties of skin colors.

It was a cornucopia of smutty goodness and she couldn't tear her eyes away. In fact, she couldn't speak either, mostly because her tongue had hit the floor. Her feet took advantage of her frozen brain, taking her to the interior door, where she wanted to press her face up against the glass.

Luckily, someone buzzed her in before she could.

They all knew her. After all, her job required her to work closely with the security firm, and therein lay her deepest, darkest problem.

Working closely with Archer Hunt was dangerous in oh so many, *many* ways, not the least of which was their history, something she did her best to never think about.

She was greeted with variations on "Hey, Elle" and "Mornin'" and then they all went their separate ways, leaving her alone with their fearless leader.

Archer.

It'd been a long time since they'd let themselves be alone. In fact, she always actively sought out ways to *not* be alone with him, and given how successful she'd been, she could only figure he'd been doing the same.

Not looking particularly bothered by this unexpected development, Archer met her gaze straight on. He hadn't unloaded his weapons or his shirt and stood there in full utility combat gear, complete with a Glock on one hip, a stun gun on the other, and a pistol strapped to a thigh. His Army hat was backward on his head. The handle of a butterfly knife stuck out of a pocket in his cargoes and he had two sets of cuffs strapped to his belt. An urban warrior, wired for sound with a two-way and a Kevlar vest strapped across his chest and back, telling Elle that wherever they'd been, he hadn't just come back from Disneyland.

She managed to be both horrified and turned on at the same time. But if life had taught her one thing the hard way, it was how to hide her thoughts and emotions, so she carefully rolled up her tongue.

The corner of Archer's mouth quirked, like maybe he could read her mind. But he didn't say a word, instead seeming perfectly content to stand there all badass and wait her out. And she knew from experience that he *could* wait her out, until the end of time if need be.

So of course, she caved and spoke first. "Long morning already?"

"Long night," he said.

He was big and tough, and frustrating beyond measure for so many reasons, not the least of which was her very secret crush on him, uncomfortably balanced on the fact that she owed him her life.

Unconcerned with any of that, he began to unload his weapons. Most of the jobs he took on were routine: criminal, corporate, and insurance investigations along with elite security contracts, surveillance, fraud, and corporate background checks. But some weren't routine at all, like the forensic investigations, the occasional big bond bounty hunting, government contract work . . . all with the potential to be dangerous if not life threatening.

In contrast, the security contract he held on this building surely seemed tame and mild in comparison, but she knew it was a favor to Spence.

"We have a problem," she said.

He arched a brow, the equivalent a long-winded query from anyone else.

She rolled her eyes and found herself in a defensive pose, hands on hips. "The emergency exit signs—"

"Already taken care of," he said.

"Okay, but Mr. Nottingham—"

"Also taken care of."

She took a deep, purposefully calming breath. It was hard to look right at him because he was very tall. At five foot seven, she was nowhere close to petite but even she barely came up to his shoulders. She hated that he had such a height advantage during their arguments. And this *was* going to be an argument.

"So what happened?" she asked. "Why did the lights go out like that, all at once?"

"Squirrels."

"Excuse me?"

At her tone, his piercing eyes flashed a disturbingly intense combination of green and light brown, reflecting the fact that he'd seen the worst of the worst and was capable of fighting it with his bare hands. She got that the edge of danger and testosterone coming off him in waves attracted the opposite sex like bees to honey but at the moment she'd like to stomp on his size thirteen Bates. Especially since he didn't repeat himself, and tired of the macho show, she poked him in the chest with her finger. His pec didn't give at all. *Stupid muscles.* "Listen," she said. "I've got pissed-off tenants, a man in the hospital, and a signed contract from you guaranteeing the safety of the people in this building. So I'm going to need you to do more than stand there all tall, dark, and silently brooding on this one, Archer, and tell me what the hell is going on, preferably using more than one word at a time."

"You want to be careful how you speak to me, Elle," he said.

The man was impenetrable. A virtual island. And he

didn't like being questioned, she knew that much. But she also knew the only way to deal with him was to hold her own. He didn't respect cowards. "Fine," she said. "Will you *pretty please* tell me what the hell is going on?"

At that he looked very slightly amused, probably because she was the only one who ever dared to push him. "Last fall I told you that you had a squirrel colony going on in the roof," he said. "I said that you needed to hire someone to block off the holes left behind by woodpeckers from the year before or you were going to have problems. You assured me you'd handled it."

"Because the landscapers assured me they'd take care of it."

He shrugged a broad shoulder. "Either they blew you off or they didn't do it correctly. An entire colony of squirrels moved into the walls and had a party. Last night they hit the electrical room, where they ate through some wires."

Well, hell. No wonder he was giving her bad 'tude. He was right. This wasn't on him at all.

It was on *her*. "What happened to the squirrels?" she asked.

"Probably dead in the walls."

She blinked. "Are you telling me I killed a bunch of squirrels?"

His mouth quirked. "What do you think the landscapers would've done? Sent them on a vacay to the Bahamas?"

"Okay," she said, letting out a long exhale. "Thanks for the explanation." She turned to go.

His hand caught her, long fingers wrapping around her elbow and causing all sorts of unwelcome sensations as he pulled her back around.

"What?" she asked.

"Waiting for my apology."

"Sure," she said agreeably. "When hell freezes over." She lifted her chin, grateful for her four-inch heels so that she could almost, kind of, not quite look him in the eyes. "I'm in charge of this building, Archer, which means I'm in charge of everything that happens in it. I'm also in charge of everyone who works *for* this building."

He cocked his head, looking amused again. "You want to be the boss of me, Elle?" he asked softly.

"I *am* the boss of you."

Now he outright smiled and her breath caught. Damn, stupid, sexy smile. And then there was The Body. Yes, she thought of it in capital letters, it deserved the respect. "If you don't want to be walking funny tomorrow," she said, "you'll stop invading my personal-space bubble."

Complete bravado and they both knew it. She'd only been at this job for a year and it'd come as a surprise to her that he'd been in the building at all. An unfortunate coincidence. Before that it'd been years since they'd had any contact, but she still knew enough to get that no one got the better of him.

He was quick, light on his feet, and physically strong. But that wasn't what made him so dangerous to her. No, it was his sharp intelligence, his quick wit, how he was willing to go as dark as he needed to in order to do what he thought was right.

And then there was the biggie—the way he had of making her feel shockingly alive.

He did as she asked and stepped back but not before pausing to make sure they both knew who was in control here, and it most definitely wasn't her.

No one did intimidation like Archer, and in his line of work he could be in a coma and still intimidate everyone in the room. He had muscles on top of muscles but didn't look beefed up like a body builder might. Instead his body seemed lean and seriously badass, with caramel skin that strayed from light to golden to mocha latte depending on what the season was, giving him a look of indeterminable origin.

And sexiness.

It worked for him, allowing him to fit in to just about any situation. Handy on the job, she imagined. But with her he was careful. Distant. And yet she'd seen the way he sometimes looked at her, and on the rare occasion when he'd touched her, like when he guided her through a door with his hand low on her back, he let himself linger. There was always a shocking and baffling yearning beyond both the glances and the touches.

That, or it was all just wishful thinking.

Not that it mattered since he still held back with her. The problem was she yearned too. Yearned for him to see her as a woman, strong and capable enough to stand at his side.

But after what they'd been through, she knew that would never happen. She turned away, annoyed by how her entire body had gone on high alert as always, every inch of her seeming to hum beneath the surface.

She should have just emailed him.

He waited until she got to the door before he spoke, "I've got a job I need your help on."

"No," she said.

He just looked at her.

She took online college classes at the crack of dawn. Her job was demanding and took up a solid eight hours a day. At night she studied, fighting for her ever elusive accounting degree. Someday she was going to run her own accounting firm and be badass too, just in a different way than Archer. She was going to be a stable, respectable badass—in great shoes. But in the meantime, she worked herself half into the grave just to keep her head above water.

Problem was, school was expensive, very expensive. As was living in San Francisco. As were great shoes. Plus good jobs didn't grow on trees. The one she'd had before this had turned out to be a nightmare. She felt lucky here, and although she was paid very decently, college was breaking her bank. To help fund herself, she took the occasional job with Archer when he needed a woman on a job. A distraction usually, but sometimes he prevailed on her other skills, skills she'd honed a lifetime ago.

"It's a challenging job," he said, knowing exactly how to pique her interest, damn him. "Need an ID on a guy, and if it's our man, we need a distraction while we . . . *borrow* his laptop, the one he never lets out of his sight."

Hmm. Definitely a challenge. "I don't suppose he's the type you could just walk up to and ask his name," she said.

His mouth curved in a small smile. "Let's just say I'm not someone who would interest him."

"No? So who would?" she asked.

"A hot blonde with legs for days in a short, tight dress."

Heat pooled in her belly and spread outward. Dammit.

"One with the stickiest pickpocket fingers I've ever met," he added.

With a low laugh—dammit, was there anything sexier than a man who knew you to the bone?—she made it to the outer reception area. She'd just reached for the front door when it opened and she collided with someone.

The man caught her, keeping her upright. "I'm so sorry. Are you alright?"

"I'm fine," she said. In his early thirties, he was about her height, medium build, and in a very nice suit. He also had a nice smile, a *kind* smile, and more than a little male interest in his expression.

"Mike Penham," he said, offering her a hand. "I'm a client of Archer's."

"Elle Wheaton." She smiled. "Not a client."

"Ah, a mysterious woman," he said with a smile.

"No, just a busy one." She shot one last look at Archer—a mistake because his gaze was inscrutable and on her as always, and she felt her stupid heart do a stupid somersault in her chest as he came into the front room, moving with his usual liquid grace in spite of still being armed for a third-world skirmish.

"Mike," he said in greeting to the man who'd just arrived. "Come on back." He looked at Elle. "Tonight then?"

Since she'd never yet figured out how to say no to the hot bastard, she nodded. And for a single beat, the mask fell from his eyes and his golden green gaze warmed as he nodded back.

And then she shut the door between them.

Accidentally on Purpose
Chapter 2

#AccidentallyOnPurpose

"DAMN, SHE'S SMOKIN' hot. Is she available?"

Archer heard Mike's question about Elle but he didn't take his gaze off her as she walked her sweet ass out of his office. "No."

Mike slapped his hand dramatically to his own chest. "Right through the heart, man. You've cut me right through the heart. She's got some serious fire, that one. Love that in a woman."

Yeah Elle had fire. She was like the sun. Get too close and you'd burn up . . . With a shake of his head at himself, Archer turned away, heading for his office.

"No, but seriously," Mike said, following along after him. "I've got a shot at her, right?"

"No."

Mike laughed. The guy was a walking conglomerate and a solid client who brought in business, a lot of it in fact, but that didn't mean Archer wanted him within fifty feet of Elle.

Granted, the vulnerable, scared, isolated sixteen-year-old street rat he'd once saved when he'd been a twenty-two-year-old rookie cop was not a street rat any more. Nor alone, scared, or vulnerable. She was outspoken and tough as nails.

But she wasn't available. Hell no.

Not that she was his.

He wanted her. And he wanted her bad too. But she'd worked her ass off to become the woman she was now. He knew he reminded her of bad times, and there was no way he'd risk setting her back or damaging her in any way. She'd been through enough without him muddying the waters. So they were friends.

Or maybe the more accurate description was that they *pretended* to be friends.

He entered his office and he gestured for Mike to have a seat. "Your message said you have a security problem."

"A big one," Mike said. "I think our digital division's got a leak."

"What makes you think so?"

"We had two new high-tech communication products that no one else even had a bead on. We had a scheduled presentation to a very selective, confidential client—"

"How selective?" Archer asked. "How confidential?"

Mike rolled his lips inward. "Let's just say *very*."

The US government, Archer figured, reading between the lines. "And let me guess, someone beat you to the punch."

"Our number one competitor," Mike said grimly. "But there's no way in hell that they beat us. Someone gave them the intel. From the inside."

"That's ugly."

"Yes. And now I need to stop the leak. You in?"

Archer nodded. "I'm in, but—"

"I know, I know," Mike said. "No guarantees, blah blah. I've heard the spiel, Hunt, but you've not failed me yet. Plus I'm going to pay you a whole helluva lot of money to make sure you don't fail me this time either."

Archer gave him a short nod. "Consider it done."

When Mike left, Archer set some plans into motion to get that job up and running, and then he got to work going over the plan for the night's distraction.

They'd been hired by an insurance company. Some of their clients were up in arms, claiming that they'd paid for additional services that had never been received.

It turned out that the insurance company didn't even provide those services and had no records of receiving the premiums.

Enter Hunt Investigations. Archer had dug in and found it all came down to one freelance insurance agent who'd quietly offered select—read: *rich*—clients some opportunities to upgrade. All that had been required were additional "premiums." The agent had then pocketed those additional premiums—of course without upgrading the policies.

With help from Archer's resident computer specialist, Joe, they'd located the "agent," a guy who had multiple aliases but was currently using the name Chuck Smithson. Some further research revealed that Chuck was a loner who trusted no one. He moved around between hotels and kept a cross-body messenger bag on him at all times, which most likely held his laptop and all his secrets. And since he lived in a state of paranoia and didn't back up anywhere that they could hack into, they needed that laptop for evidence.

During their research, they'd found that swindler Chuck had an additional habit—he enjoyed trolling Internet hookup sites. Archer had gotten an email earlier from Elle that she was in on the job, so they'd set up a profile for bait. Chuck had taken that bait hook, line, and sinker, and was in fact expecting to meet "Candy Cunningham" tonight for a drink.

All Archer needed Elle to do was ID Chuck and then keep him busy while they took a look in the briefcase and copied his hard drive. The evidence wouldn't be admissible in court but the insurance company didn't want to take it that far and risk the public hearing about their humiliatingly heavy losses. They just wanted Hunt Investigations to confirm their suspicions before figuring out their next step.

Archer texted his team and waited as they began to file back in, fresh from showers, various forms of caffeine in one hand, breakfast in the other.

Max was head of the pack and since he'd been with his girlfriend, Rory, for two months now—a record for him—there was a definite pep to his step. He sat across the conference table from Archer with Carl, his Doberman, at his side. Carl was a huge asset to their team but at the moment all he had on his brain was the massive donut in his master's hand.

Max shoved a huge bite of said donut into his mouth. "All set for tonight, boss," he said to Archer. "We've got entrances and exits covered and Finn's going to have all eyes on deck for us."

Finn was the owner and bartender at O'Riley's, the pub on the ground floor of the building where the distraction would take place. He also happened to be a close friend.

Archer didn't usually bring work so close to his home base but he never took chances when it came to Elle.

Never.

She was a great asset when he needed a distraction because she had a way of making a man forget he had a brain. He'd been a victim of this himself, more than once. Thing was, too many times to count she'd managed to get him information that had closed a case for him, info he couldn't have gotten without bloodshed.

She claimed to do these jobs because she loved the money. He knew that wasn't strictly true. She did love money, in the way that only someone who'd grown up without any could. But he knew that wasn't why she did it. Nope, she worked for him when he asked because she thought she owed him.

But the truth was, he owed her.

The rest of the guys got comfortable. Joe, who besides being his IT guy was also his right-hand man. Then there was Lucas, Trev, and Reyes. Their conference room was big, but so were they and the room seemed to shrink in their presence.

"Why do you smell like maple and bacon?" Joe asked Max.

"Because I'm eating a maple and bacon donut," Max said.

"No shit?"

"No shit."

Joe's stomach growled loud enough to echo off the walls.

Max blew out a sigh and tossed him a white paper bag. "You gotta share with Carl though—I promised him some."

Carl gave one sharp bark in agreement.

The rest of the guys protested, loudly.

"I want it."

"Shit, man, I'll even pay for it."

But Joe held tight to the bag, fighting the others off. When he was in the clear, he pulled out the donut, broke off a corner, and tossed it to Carl, who caught it in midair with an audible snap of his huge jaws.

"Dude," Max chided his dog, "you didn't even taste that."

Carl licked his massive chops but didn't take his eyes off Joe, his new BFF.

Joe bit into the rest of the donut. Closing his eyes, he leaned his head back and moaned.

"Maybe you need a moment alone with that thing," Archer said dryly.

"Yes. *Jesus.*"

"Right?" Max said with a smile. "I wanna marry this donut and have its babies."

This started an explicit, filthy conversation that had everyone laughing until Archer opened his laptop. Immediately all conversation and amusement faded away.

Time to get to work.

THIRTY MINUTES BEFORE the night's gig, Archer heard the outer door to his offices open and close and then soft voices.

His receptionist, Mollie, greeting someone.

A few seconds later he heard the soft *click, click, click* of heels heading his way.

Mollie wore heels. So did some of his clients. But he knew the sound of these. Even if there hadn't been attitude in every single step he would've recognized Elle's smooth, confident stride anywhere.

And if that didn't clue him in, the fact that his dick stirred was a dead giveaway.

A text from Mollie came through announcing Elle's arrival just as the woman herself knocked once on his door. She leaned against the wood, saying nothing.

She looked . . . heart-stopping. That was the thing about Elle, she was always one hundred percent put together. He'd had plenty of women in his life. He knew the effort that they put in and the mind-boggling time they took, so he had no idea how Elle did it day in and day out. But whether on the job or in her personal life, it didn't matter, she dressed like a million bucks and she never had so much as a single strand of her shoulder length blonde hair out of place. In fact, there'd only been one time in the eleven years he'd known her when she hadn't been on her game and she sure as hell wouldn't thank him for the reminder of that long ago, fateful night.

Earlier this morning she'd been in a power-red suit dress that had screamed success, even at the crack of dawn. She'd changed into a killer little black dress, emphasis on *little*. Her heels defied gravity with sexy little straps around her ankles and bows at the back, and her expression said she ate men for breakfast, lunch, and dinner.

She did a slow twirl and he stopped breathing as he slowly rose from his chair. "Holy shit, Elle."

"I wasn't going for holy shit. I was going for sophisticated sexy."

"Copy that," he said. "But you're also one hundred percent holy shit. You're also a walking heart attack and aneurism—an all-in-one special."

"Good. I was worried that maybe I look a little bit too much like I belong on Post Street."

He looked her over again, enjoying the view way too much. "Post Street's looking good."

She rolled her eyes. "You should check out the corner of Post and *Kiss My Ass*."

He grinned and strolled over to her. She smelled like a million bucks, making him want to press his face into her hair, or better yet her neck so he could inhale her like she was his own maple and bacon donut. Instead, he handed her an earpiece. "Comms. We'll all be connected. There'll be constant eyes on you too. The guys are already in place. Our mark isn't known to be dangerous or armed but—"

"You're not taking any chances with me yadda yadda," she said impatiently, taking the earpiece. "I've heard the spiel before. I'm not a special snowflake, Archer. If I was, I wouldn't be here—you wouldn't allow it."

All true. But he could no more curb his insane need to keep her protected and safe than he could stop breathing. It'd always been like that for him with her.

She put in the earpiece and give him a little nod.

"Okay," he said. "So—"

"I've read the file you emailed me," she interrupted. "I'm going in as Candy Cunningham, the girl Chuck swiped for and thinks is tonight's hookup. I'm to get in, ID him, hold his attention until you guys do your thing with the laptop that's hopefully in his briefcase, and then get out."

"And get out fast, Elle. I don't want him to know you're—"

"Not Candy," she said. "I think I know what I'm doing by now. You ready to do this or do you need to freshen up your lipstick?"

Since she was now wired for sound and so was Archer, he heard the snickers and snorts from his men in his ear. He didn't bother to respond. He could and did demand their respect. But he was under no such illusions when it came to controlling Elle.

They took the elevator in silence. Elle stared at the

doors. Archer stared at Elle. He had no idea how the dress was containing her full breasts with that low, plunging vee. Every move she made, they strained to escape.

What felt like a year later, the elevator doors finally opened. He caught Elle's hand and waited until she met his gaze. "You've got fifteen minutes to gain his attention or walk out," he said. "After that we go to Plan B."

"Which is?"

"A plan that doesn't involve you."

"In that dress, she's only going to need one minute," Joe said in Archer's ear from his vantage point in the courtyard.

"I'd put money down on fifteen seconds," Reyes said.

"Shut it," Archer said.

Radio silence followed this directive.

Elle snorted and walked off, her heels clicking over the cobblestones as she passed the fountain in the center of the courtyard and entered the pub.

Archer took a moment to shake it off—around her he had to do that a helluva lot—and followed. He was going in as a patron and would be guarding her sexy ass.

O'Riley's was one half-bar, one-half seated dining. The walls were dark wood that gave an old-world feel to the place. Brass lanterns hung from the rafters and rustic baseboards finished the look that said *sit your tired ass down, order good food and spirits, and be merry.*

Catching sight of Elle heading toward the bar wasn't difficult, people parted like the Red Sea for her, making room. She settled herself on a barstool right next to Chuck Smithson and nodded to the bartender.

Finn.

"Nonalcoholic," Archer murmured.

Finn, also wired, nodded even though they'd already gone through all this. On the job there was never any alcohol allowed.

Elle waited for her drink and then took a sip, all without looking at their guy.

Chuck sat on the stool next to her. He was five foot four, wiry, and with his wrinkled academic-looking clothes and thick black-rimmed glasses he was either a hipster wannabe or making a play for imitating a slightly grown-up Harry Potter. His feet didn't touch the floor, instead they were hooked into a rung of the barstool, his briefcase settled between his boots. He'd swiveled to watch, actually stare, at Elle, and when she slowly turned as if eyeing the room, he straightened, pushed his glasses higher on the bridge of his nose and sent her a hopeful smile.

She gave him one in return, a sugary sweet smile that Archer sure as hell had never seen aimed his way before and which had Chuck nearly falling off his stool.

"Man, she's something," Joe whispered in their ears.

"You're drooling," Max said.

"We're all drooling," Lucas said. "She's a walking boner."

"Silence," Archer ordered quietly and they all shut the hell up.

Still looking sweet and somehow demure despite the sexy-as-hell getup, Elle leaned into Chuck. Archer watched closely, fascinated because he knew she could pick a pocket in a few seconds flat right in front of his eyes and he wouldn't even see it.

"Chuck?" Elle whispered.

Her pic had been on her bio but the guy swallowed hard and nodded, his eyes lit like he'd just discovered it was Christmas morning. "Candy?"

Elle bit her lower lip, managing to look a little shy. "Would you mind showing me your ID?" she asked. "You wouldn't believe the number of creepers I have to weed through."

"I bet," Chuck said sympathetically. "It's because you're so beautiful."

This guy was eating out of the palm of her hand. She wasn't even going to have to use her skills. Archer found himself smiling at her cleverness and shaking his head in awe. He loved watching her in action, which he didn't get to see often.

She hadn't made a secret of the fact that she didn't like him all that much. Not that he blamed her. She associated him with a very bad part of her past, plus he knew she thought he was too bossy and a control freak—both of which happened to be true.

But it took one to know one.

Chuck hopped of his stool and pulled a wallet from his back pocket.

Elle, smart enough to kick off her high heels to cut her own height down before standing up too, gathered her shoes by the strap, hanging them off a finger. She then leaned into Chuck to look at his ID, letting her hair fall into his face and, Archer was pretty sure, also letting her breast brush against the guy's arm.

Chuck swallowed hard, blinking when Elle lifted her beaming face to his. "Nice to meet you, Chuck Smithson," she said.

"ID confirmation," Max said into his comms from where he sat at the bar two spots over, appearing to be lost in the basketball game on the TV behind the bar. "I'm in place to move in."

Now all Elle had to do was keep Chuck distracted from his briefcase while he did.

"Can we dance?" Elle asked, shy. Timid.

Archer didn't have a type when it came to women. He liked them in all shapes and sizes and in a wide variety of personalities. But shy and timid had never done much for him.

Until right that minute. Even knowing it was a damn act, knowing that Elle didn't have a shy or timid bone in her body, he wanted to go over there, haul her in tight, and comfort her. It was such a shocking urge he nearly missed what came next.

"Uh." Chuck blinked up at Elle, still several inches shorter than she. "I'm not much of a dancer—"

"Oh, no worries," she said sweetly, "everyone's got a dancer deep inside him."

"But—"

"Please?" she asked softly, batting those baby blues.

Chuck downed his drink. "For liquid courage," he said, gesturing to Finn for another.

"Make it a double," Archer instructed Finn.

"I'll lead," Elle promised Chuck as he tossed back the second drink. Winding an arm in one of his, she pulled him away from the bar.

"But my stuff . . ." Twisting back, he eyed his briefcase on the floor.

"It's safe here." Elle looked at Finn behind the bar. "Right?"

"Absolutely," Finn said.

"But—"

But nothing. The poor dumb fucker never knew what hit him. As Elle led him by the balls to the dance floor, keeping Chuck's back to the bar, Joe moved in, smoothly grabbed the briefcase, and vanished.

On the small, crowded dance floor, Elle began to move, shimmying that body of hers, dazzling Chuck—and every other man in the place—into an openmouthed stupor.

Not Archer. No, he was in heart failure because if she wasn't careful she was going to come right out of that dress. "Joe, report," he said, rubbing his left eye, which had started to twitch.

"We're an inch from a nipple-gate situation," Max said in a reverent, hopeful whisper.

Archer made a mental note to kill him later. "*Joe.*"

"Need three more minutes."

Shit. The seconds crawled by, while on the dance floor Chuck had moved up against Elle and was grinning ear to ear as he tried to keep up with her.

As if anyone could.

"Done," Joe finally said, and Archer breathed for the first time in the longest three minutes of his life.

"Copied the hard drive," Joe said, and then in the next beat Archer watched as he smoothly replaced the briefcase beneath Chuck's barstool.

Not two seconds later Chuck turned from the dance floor, his gaze seeking and finding his briefcase, still under his barstool.

"All done, boss," Joe said. "Oh and the guy's got a handful of different IDs on him as well as the laptop. Scanned everything."

Score. "Elle," Archer said. "Make your exit."

The music was loud, so was the pub. People were having a great time. And apparently Chuck was one of them because his liquid courage had clearly kicked in. Some confidence too because he kept trying to get his hands all over Elle as they moved together to the beat.

"You're so pretty!" Chuck yelled up to Elle's face.

She smiled.

"No, I mean like . . . porn pretty!" He was still yelling. "I'm kind of a connoisseur, so I'd know! Have you ever thought about it? You'd make millions!" He grinned. "Usually when I get drunk, I talk loud, like *really* loud! But I'm not doing that now because you don't even look scared!"

"You ever miss being a cop in moments like this?" Max asked conversationally in Archer's ear. "Cuz then you could go arrest that fucker."

No, Archer didn't miss being a cop. As for what he *did* miss from that old life—his dad for one, no matter how hard-assed the guy had been—he'd shoved it deep and moved on. The real question was *why the hell was Elle still dancing?* He'd given her orders to move out. Making his way through the crowd, he hit the dance floor and tapped Chuck on the shoulder.

The guy turned and looked up, up, up into Archer's face. "Erm—" he squeaked out. With a gulp, he relinquished his hold on Elle like she was a hot potato and scampered off like a rat into the night. After stopping for his briefcase, of course.

Elle bent to slip back into her heels.

Apparently she needed the armor with Archer. Slipping an arm around her waist to give her the support she needed to buckle herself into the FMPs, he waited until she straightened then said, "What the fuck was that?"

"Me doing my job," she said in a *duh* voice.

"Since when is dirty dancing with a felon your job?"

She narrowed her fierce eyes. "You told me to get close to him. You told me to ID him and then keep him distracted, whatever it takes."

"Okay, *no*," he said. "I absolutely did not say *whatever it takes.*"

She glared up at him.

"*What?*" he asked.

"Nothing." Her voice was ice.

"Oh boy," Joe muttered in Archer's ear. "When a woman says 'nothing' in that tone, it most definitely means something and you should be wearing a cup to finish that conversation. Just sayin'."

Archer put a finger to his eye before it twitched right

out of his head. "I told you to make your exit," he said to Elle with what he thought was remarkable calm while ignoring Joe, who was a dead man walking anyway. "When I tell you something, Elle, I expect you to listen."

He heard a collective sucking in of air through his comms and ignored that too.

"Wow," Elle finally said.

"Okay," Max piped up. "I have a girlfriend now so I know this one. When Rory says 'wow' like that, it's not a compliment. It means she's thinking long and hard on how and when I'll pay for my stupidity."

"Agreed," Joe said. "She's simply expressing amazement that a man can be such an idiot. Abort mission, boss. I repeat. *Abort. Mission.*"

Shit. Archer ripped out his earpiece and then did the same to Elle's, stuffing both in his pocket.

She shrugged and walked away, leaving him on the dance floor. Watching her go, an odd feeling cranked over in his chest. Irritation, he decided. Frustration. The woman got to him like no one else.

And yet he'd kept tabs on her, watching her back. He couldn't explain why, but apparently old habits died hard.

Did she ever think about that night? She'd never made a single reference to it, not once. And he'd never brought it up, not wanting to bring her back to a bad place.

When he walked off the dance floor and headed toward the bar, she was there, right there, picking up the wrap she'd left. Something fell from it and hit the floor.

They both crouched low at the same time but Archer

beat her to it. When he realized what he held, he lifted his head and stared at her in shock.

It was the small pocket knife he'd given her all those years ago.

Which meant she *did* think about that night.

About the Author

New York Times bestselling author **JILL SHALVIS** lives in a small town in the Sierras full of quirky characters. Any resemblance to the quirky characters in her books is, um, mostly coincidental. Look for Jill's bestselling, award-winning books wherever romances are sold, and visit her website for a complete book list and daily blog detailing her city-girl-living-in-the-mountains adventures.

Discover great authors, exclusive offers, and more at hc.com.

MAR - - 2017